PROTOTYPE

The Unchipped series:
THE MEETING: AN UNCHIPPED SHORT STORY
UNCHIPPED: KAARINA
UNCHIPPED: WILLIAM
UNCHIPPED: ENYD
UNCHIPPED: LUNA
UNCHIPPED: THE RESORT
CHIPPED: LAURA
CHIPPED: DENNIS
CHIPPED: MARGARET
CHIPPED: JOVAN
CHIPPED: THE REVENANT
DECHIPPED: KRISTIAN
DECHIPPED: MARIA
DECHIPPED: OWENA
DECHIPPED: IRIS
DECHIPPED: THE DOWNLOAD
RECHIPPED: CITY OF SERBIA
RECHIPPED: CITY OF ENGLAND
RECHIPPED: CITY OF CALIFORNIA
RECHIPPED: CITY OF FINLAND
RECHIPPED: THE BUTTON

The Unchipped Omnibus series:
UNCHIPPED
CHIPPED
DECHIPPED
RECHIPPED

The Machina Deus series:
SERF GIRL
FAMA GIRL
SLUM GIRL

PROTOTYPE Y (**StandaloneNovella**)

COMING SOON!
THE ISLANDER (**Standalone Novel**)

PROTOTYPE Y

TAYA DEVERE

CONTENT WARNING: SA. While not a main theme of the book, some readers may want to read the reviews or have a friend check out the book before reading.

DVM PRESS

DVM Press
Vaakunatie 16 D 14,
20780 Kaarina, Suomi-Finland

www.dvmpress.com
www.tayadevere.com

First Edition

For information about special discounts available for bulk purchases, sales promotions, fund-raising and educational needs, contact sales@dvmpress.com

ISBN 978-952-7601-05-1 First Ebook Edition
ISBN 978-952-7601-06-8 First Print PPB Edition
ISBN 978-952-7601-04-4 First Audiobook Edition

Cover Design © 2025 by 17 Studio Book Design - www.17studiobookdesign.com

Editing by Christopher Scott Thompson and Lauren H. Brooks

To the women who have stepped out of line.

CONTENTS

PROTOTYPE Y

CHAPTER 1

Wires and soft tissue poke out from the detached arm I'm holding. Artificial blood and cooling fluid trickle together across the back of my hand, her light-green skin cold and de-activated in my firm grip.

It's G's arm, not my own. My brain knows this. Two arms, two legs, a torso, and a head—my body still has it all. Normally, this knowledge would bring some calm to my overheated vessel—not today. This is not a normal day. Not a normal situation.

I scan the room. Seven humans stand in a half circle in front of me, the four older males naked, the three younger ones shaking in their red, blue, and yellow skirts and matching tank tops.

Desperate to push aside the data and the hormone frenzy crowding my skull and body, I focus on controlling the pheromone vials in my chest and stomach. I run a quick inventory.

Compassion. Amusement. Curiosity.

Is it enough to get past this hostile group of men?

The words *DARK ROOM* flicker on the neon-orange sign above the low staircase leading upstairs. The only sounds filling the musky and humid air of the dimly lit basement room are the steady beat of a low-key bass and the breathing of seven disoriented men. One of the naked ones reaches for a towel. The rest lock their widened eyes on the arm I'm holding.

I'm surrounded by enclosed cubicle rooms, rubber gadgets, beds, swing sets, and dismembered Prototypes. The smell of testosterone, sweat, and alcohol clings onto my body, which is smudged all over with blood and cooling fluid. Inundated with bodily fluids, this space is an overkill of data that skews my base readings. Sensory overload isn't new to me, but again, things are different this time around.

My brain recaps the plan.

Bring G's arm.

Grab a heart.

Get back to the truck.

I don't need to run a probability scan to know my odds aren't great. One Prototype against seven humans—seven and half, if you count the poor towel-boy slowly drowning in his own blood by my feet.

"Psst, Mike," the man with a towel whispers.

"The fuck, man? Don't use my real name here."

"Can you shoot it?"

"The gun's upstairs. You know Buck doesn't allow any firearms down here."

"I say the towel-boys should take it down."

The room falls silent, the bass pounding against the bottom of my bare feet. Why the men won't simply turn around and leave is beyond me.

"Take it...but how, sir?" the towel-boy in a red skirt says, scratching his head. "None of us know how to fight."

"Sure you do," Mike says. "I bet you're really good at it too."

While the boy wearing yellow starts trembling violently, the one in blue says, "Tha-that's not really a thing, sir. You're just ga-gaslamping us."

"What?" the boy in red snaps. "No, you ding-dong. It's *gaslighting—*"

"Quit your fucking arguing," Mike says, "and go rip the goddamn thing to pieces. Your friend made the error of going after it alone. There's three of you. You'll be fine."

I glance at the towel-boy on the floor, a hollow sensation in my chest. The boy's round face with wispy facial hair is typical of a human male below the age of thirty. Lungs crushed by a two-hundred-pound Prototype, he's no longer gurgling, but lying dead on the filthy floor.

Let me walk G out of here without a fight.

That's all you had to do.

As I watch him, my hormone frenzy reactivates. Killing an innocent male has pushed my system deeper into the loop of inexperienced, uncontrollable turmoil. I dig through my archives and move the snippet of elementary data to short-term storage. Maybe reminding my system of its basic functionality—the neurobiology of chemical communication—will finally stop the glitching.

Pheromones influence those around you.

Hormones affect your own body.

You control their feelings—not the other way around.

Despite the gentle reminder, none of my vials clink into life. Whatever liquids remain in my system continue to vibrate uselessly to the rhythm of the bass.

Amusement, activate.

Nothing clicks, moves, or evaporates inside me. All I feel is the swarm of organic sorrow, guilt, and regret.

Activate. Amusement. Immediately.

Nothing.

Curiosity, activate.

My vial system remains perfectly quiet.

The air is thick with fear-laced sweat as the men fidget and scan the room for possible weapons. I'm running out of time. My brain locates the one vial I'm desperate to save for the beast that waits upstairs. But then, if my body never makes it up there...

What good is the vial to me if I'm deactivated—dead?

Activate compassion.

Clink.

A hint of warmth spreads inside my chest, radiating to my stomach, filling my body with a light softness reminiscent of cotton balls, feathers, and satin. The pheromone cloud evaporates and spreads around me.

Body, approach.

I step forward. Enter the cloud of intensifying fear. Just as I'm getting close, two of the naked men flee up the stairs, while the one in a towel sidesteps to the wall. A *clank* echoes through the room. One by one, the dim lights around the cubicles, couches, and corpses switch off, blanketing us in darkness.

My system stops for new base readings.

"Are you *insane*?" Mike grumbles.

"Its eyes. I don't think it can hear or smell. I think it can only see."

"It's a murder machine gone rogue, not a real human with real senses. Just because it doesn't have a mouth—"

"Oh, so you're the fucking Prototype specialist all of a sudden?"

"Whatever, man. Either shut the fuck up or run after your wimpy-ass friends." Mike gestures into the darkness. "Like I said, the boys can handle it."

A soft rustling of fabric reaches my ears. The towel-boys are trembling. Only the boy in red stays somewhat calm, his eyes tracing my figure in the dark. As their adrenaline and cortisol levels intensify, so does the havoc within me.

"But sir..." the boy in a yellow skirt says. "Ma-maybe it'll just..."

"Spit it out, rag boy."

"Maybe it'll just let us leave?" the boy in a blue skirt finishes his whimpering friend's thought.

Mike scoffs. His half-nude companion rolls his eyes. I can see their expressions as clearly as if we stood in broad daylight.

"Oh, but sure," Mike says. "Just say pretty-please three times real fast, and the nice bot lady shuts itself down and sends us on our merry way."

"Sir," the red skirt says, "all we're saying is that it didn't hurt Luke until he accidentally ripped off its bot friend's arm—"

"That's enough," Mike says. "No self-respecting man walks away from a fight. And no, I shouldn't just 'do it myself, then.' You work here, I'm a paying customer. This asshole doll has ruined enough of my day off. Shut it down, now."

"I already told you, sir," the red skirt says. "None of us know how to fi—"

"Don't fucking sir me, boy. Buck told me that all you little fuckholes do in your spare time is play *Burn of Vengeance* until your eyes bleed. How hard can it be to repeat fight scenes you've seen fifteen thousand times?"

I scan my archives for the keyword *Burn of Vengeance*. As the three towel-boys finally lift their trembling hands and approach me with their doomed little hearts racing, I've downloaded every fight scene from their favorite videogame into my short-term memory.

"Fine," the boy in red says. "Turn the light back on. Raymond and Levi will take it down."

In shock, the blue and yellow skirts glance at their confident-sounding friend.

At the startling *clank* sound and the return of the dim light, the first boy grumbles, turns, and comes in at me, his blue skirt flapping against his flimsy frame. My system reads him with ease. *Sumo hand slap*.

I move aside, grab him with my free hand, then use G's leaking arm to hug him close to me. The gentle cloud of *compassion* evaporates from me, mixing with his anxiety-laced fear. I hold him close, my grip tight.

Take it in, you poor little thing. Just let it happen.

The boy in yellow lunges at me. *Hurricane kick,* my

system reads and spins me around. I block his kick with my calf, the unexpected impact sending him crashing to the floor. Screaming, he reaches for my left calf, his teeth sinking into my bone-like structure.

I feel the vial drip faster inside me, a cloud of *compassion* closing in, surrounding me and the two boys.

The muscles of the first boy relax. He moves back in my hold, his intent stare carefully investigating my face.

The bite on my calf hardens. I stomp and kick the shaking boy off my leg. Pieces of teeth clatter onto the floor as he flies backward and lands against the stairs, hitting his head. His yellow skirt flaps wildly in the stream of air from the AC.

Oh. That's not what I—

The boy in my arms starts sobbing. I let go of him, but his body remains glued to mine. "I'm sorry Luke ripped your friend apart. He never... We don't even like how... It's just... I need this job to..."

His words give me pause. A warm wave runs through me, then a shivering chill, my head and chest filling with a hollow sensation as I stare into his tear-filled eyes. For a moment, all that's left in the room is him and me. My focus slips even further away from my wildly glitching pheromones.

Clink.

I don't need to locate which vial drips inside me to know it's the wrong one. A bad one. Truly a detrimental choice. I know, because the liquid in this vial is at its max. It's never been used before—for good reason.

Oh...shoot.

I let go of the sobbing boy and shove him toward the stairs. With adrenaline-driven force, he pushes through Mike and the man in a towel. The scent of blood tickling my nose, I watch him climb over his freshly dead friend and scramble up the stairs toward safety.

Mike, red skirt, and the man in the towel stare at me for 3.2 seconds. The adrenaline and cortisol levels in the room plummet as the two older men disappear up and through the doorway below the *DARK ROOM* sign.

Kneeling on the stairs, the boy in red places two fingers on his dead friend's neck.

You look for a pulse.

You won't find one.

Ten seconds of desperate searching, and he looks up, his furious eyes locked with mine. I don't need to read his system to know what his brain has decided.

He's not leaving.

He wants revenge.

The rattle of liquids inside my chest pauses as the song changes. Once the bass returns, I feel the accidentally activated vial vibrate out of control, liquid dripping and evaporating faster from my system.

The boy steps down the stairs. His eyes fill with focus and hunger, like he's a feral *Mephitidae* and me his rodent prey.

I take a step back, trying to keep my distance.

He strides faster toward my retreating body and through the cloud of *arrogance* emitting from me.

"Game over, you filthy NPC bitch."

He reaches me, jumps at me. I spin around, and he lands on my back. With my free hand, I reach for him, try to pull him off, but he sticks to my blue skin like a blood-hungry *Hirudinea*. My system reads his videogame-based attacks, while *arrogance* fills the air around our spinning bodies.

Tiger knee.

Split punch.

Wrestler's spin.

His animal-like scream mixes in with the electric tinning in my head. I wait for his pheromone-driven aggression to slowly tire his flimsy body. His punches turn into clawing and scratching. His spitting and screaming become violent crying.

Clink.

Which...vial was that?

The organic hormone chaos swarms through my

system. Never before have I lost control of my system in such a catastrophic way. As if my pheromones have grown limbs and a will of their own, like I'm turning into a shell-flinging *Octopoda*.

Arrogance and *frustration* clinging onto his body, he sinks his teeth into my shoulder while his two hands rip apart the soft tissue of my lower back.

I lift G's green arm, snap it back. The wires and heavy Prototype meat slap him with a loud *plop*. He falls with a *thunk*.

I turn and smack the arm across his upper body, while my struggling system backfires, sucking in his arrogance, frustration, fear.

Deactivate, you wasteful...

The arm whacks his waist.

...useless, sack of...

The last blow smashes his head in.

...human scum.

At the sound of his skull breaking, I stop. I cradle the cold, green arm against my body. I hear the AC running and the red skirt flapping against the slim, lifeless corpse. Those are the only sounds while I stand, waiting for the beast.

The song changes. A new low-key rhythm vibrates against my bare feet. I bring G's green, damaged-beyond-repair arm up to eyelevel, and stare at it with a calming hollowness spreading inside me.

Todd can't use this.

Sorry, G.

I get 5.8 seconds to cool down my system until a set of footsteps drags across the upstairs floor above me. Gunpowder's subtle scent is clear in my nose, as Buck hauls his three-hundred-pound body toward the stairs.

His rumbling voice reverberates through the ceiling. "Okay, B, G, Y, whatever your model. I suppose your maker never told you, so here's a quick and dirty history lesson. A decade ago, the last sentient woman on Earth died. On this day, the human female became irrevocably extinct. Unpopular opinion or not"—he loads his gun—"I say let's keep it that way."

I kneel, set G's arm to rest on the floor, and cover it with a towel.

This won't be the end of us.

My hands fumble for and locate the still-wet, still-warm leg under the red skirt. I grab a limb and claim my weapon with one fast rip. Left hand holding onto the thigh, the right on the ankle, my eyes lock on the flickering sign, my ears focused on the slow approach of sluggish footsteps.

Vials. Inventory.

Clink-clink-clink.

I listen to the vials mindlessly activating. The inventory is executed in 2.3 seconds.

2/5 ounces of disgust.
3/5 ounces of boredom.
A few drops of leftover compassion and amusement.
That's all I have left to fight the big boss.

CHAPTER 2
48 HOURS BEFORE BIG BOSS

He's elbow deep in my stomach. My body lies still while his fingers move up and fumble for the vial closest to my chest. A thick shred of my midriff moves along with his jerks and pulls, tickling the sides of my ribs. The irritating, vinegary scent of superglue clings to me and the two men around the operating table.

The gaping hole in my upper body gives him easy access to most of the vials, but not all. With a neutral expression on my face, my brain focuses on the small dents on the vehicle's rust-covered ceiling instead of his fiddling fingers. He moves the soft tissue aside. Strokes the small adjustable slots where the twenty-seven vials plug into my system—and finally grasps what he seeks. A faint *clink,* and the ampoule is out.

Disgust. That might be the right vial to describe all this. Or, as a human would word it, the right *feeling*. But my vessel—the body, the brain, the system—is not a real human. Not an actual woman. My body can't feel pain whenever his rough fingers enter my gaping torso to fill, alter, or optimize the vials. My brain isn't sophisticated enough to use, process, or understand *feelings* on my own.

"Just as I thought," my maker says, his voice as hoarse and listless as usual. My eyes don't need to find his face to know his large nostrils are widening, making him look like *Equus caballus*. "Craving's actually a bit low. Hey Todd, get me a new vial from the freezer drawer, would you? Let's fill her up with, well, everything. Make the doses double intensity and grab some triple-strength compassion while you're at it. Tonight's patron is a real namby-pamby."

But Todd, my maker's assistant, doesn't move. My ears hear him scratching his close-shaven head. Instead of hurrying to the travel refrigerator by the back doors, his feet stay put.

The truck's A/C hums faintly. The engine is left on, which means we're behind schedule. But the job site could be a thousand miles away, and it wouldn't change a thing. These pit stops happen despite all schedules, last-minute patrons, and returning customer conversion rates. My maker's ideas for improvement overrule everything else. His attempt to become the new God and save what's left of humanity justifies the occasional postponed booking. Or that's what he says, anyway. Whether it's true, my brain wouldn't know. But if my system reads Todd's pheromones right—and it always does—he strongly disagrees.

My brain likes Todd.

Guess my body would, too, if he were a customer.

The vials clink against a metal tray. "Um, hello?" My maker's steps thump against the truck's floor. My ears register a familiar *flap* as he smacks Todd on the back of his head. "Earth to Todd?"

Todd opens his mouth but doesn't answer.

"Mother of pearl." My maker kicks the rolling stool, sending it crashing against the metal cubbies that line the truck's cargo space. "Must I do everything myself?"

With angry steps, he walks over to the back, pulls open the fridge, and rummages through the panels of ampoules. Todd moves to stand next to my body where it lies on the operating table. Rubbing the back of his head, he glances in the refrigerator's general direction, then at me, then at my maker again. My system reads his movements. His heart rate. His hormones. The micro-expressions on his face.

Fear.

Anxiety.

Confusion.

But the bundle of uneasy emotions Todd feels isn't

because of his superior smacking him. No, Todd's afraid *for me*.

My brain focuses on three specific vials, ones used during every single session:

Calmness.

Relief.

Curiosity.

But as my system tries to activate the ampoules, nothing clicks, leaks, or evaporates within me. Todd's blood pressure keeps increasing. Cortisol and adrenaline flow through his body, and there's nothing my system can do about it.

Not while it's all torn open on the operating table.

Sighing, my maker stomps over. He reaches for the stool and rolls it back to the table. My brain doesn't bother to monitor his system the way it does Todd's. Not anymore. After hundreds of readings, it simply became a meaningless task. The results were always the same.

Excitement.

Loneliness.

Fear.

Todd stays next to my body but takes a step away from his superior. The vials clink as my maker arranges them on the tray. Todd's hand scratches the side of his furrowed face, then grabs the edge of the table next to my head. My brain registers a firm yank on my midriff and a hand re-entering my torso. At the same time, my body senses Todd's pinky finger discreetly caressing the top of my hairless scalp. The gesture is a nice one. Kind. Todd would get an appreciative smile in return—if only my face had a mouth.

"Oh, Todd, Todd, Todd..." Another tug shakes my body as my maker pushes his arm deeper into me, toward my chest—toward the vials hardly ever used. "We've talked about this."

"Talked about what?" Todd asks, his hand frozen on the table.

A faint *click* comes from my chest. "Anthropomorphism. That's the word of the day. And not just today, but every single damn day since you first climbed into this vehicle and asked if it used to be a garbage truck."

The scent of Todd's fear intensifies. He says nothing. We all know this used to be a garbage truck. Just as we all know exactly what Todd's hired to do—drive it from job to job.

My brain would enjoy that, driving from A to B, though it'd prefer doing so while my maker stuffed his face with food at one of the black mold-stained diners he's so fond of. My hands would buckle and secure Todd in the seat at the back, not the other way around. My body would press the clutch pedal with my left foot. Press the brake pedal with the right. Turn the key—let my brain pick a route to its liking.

Take what the internet calls *initiative.*

"You know what you signed up for," my maker mutters to Todd. "Don't bother telling me otherwise."

"I'm not." Todd shifts his weight. "I didn't."

His rough hands grab the flappy parts of my body and spread me wider open. "Good. Now make yourself useful and hand me fresh vials of anger, craving, confusion, and horror."

For a moment, the truck falls silent. My brain reads disbelief. Todd's unwilling to do as he's told. Then, a *smack* splits the cabin's slightly musky air.

The gentle touch on my scalp is gone. Still hesitating but now forced to act, Todd reaches over me. The vials clink softly against each other as they switch hands. Tugging on me once more, my maker lowers himself to take a better look. Two hands enter me at once, pushing the missing vial into its slot faster and more forcefully than before.

"I thought we didn't use that stuff anymore," Todd says.

"Well." My maker grunts as the second vial closest to my chest slips from his fingers and pushes into my soft parts. After a moment of fishing, he grabs it and rams it into its designated place. Cursing under his breath, he sits upright and wipes his forehead. "Good thing I don't pay you to think."

Todd crosses his arms and stares into space. "You

said that high percentages in the anger-driven pheromones triggered too much testosterone and serotonin in our clientele. That you worried she might end up like our previous Prototypes."

"What, sticky and torn?" He snorts at his own joke. "Live a little, Toddy-boy. A bit of A/B testing never hurt anyone. It's called optimized customer satisfaction. Scaling for higher conversions. Or, or," he waves his hand in the air, "*customized* microtargeting."

Todd mutters, but my ears catch his words with ease. "Yes, sir."

"It's going to be a lucrative week, boy. Our first patron may be a namby-pamby, but the second one is a high-level tipping Kink and the third one, yeah, the third one's a fucking *whale*. A whale with unique preferences? Sure. A high-maintenance customer? Definitely. This egoistic schmuck even wanted me to lay down the basic research for Y's development process before he agreed to proceed with the booking. But who cares! Because when he finally proceeded, he booked our Toots for three solid hours, all bells and whistles included. So yeah, better fill it up real good."

"Unique preferences?" Todd steps over to sit by the small computer desk with a screen and a keyboard. He taps on the keys, filling the truck with cold blue light. "Sounds like a red-list candidate. At least all the ones we've crossed paths with so far have fit that profile. I'm telling you, this customer looks alarming to me. Less than ideal."

"Relax. Not only is our Toots strong as a bulldozer, but it also lacks all lady parts. Add to that her asymmetric, mouthless face and dull light-blue skin... Yeah, I think we're safe. I wouldn't touch that thing with a ten-foot pole, so neither will the patrons. Not like that, anyway."

"I'm not worried about the Kink. I'm worried about the Redlister."

Todd keeps tapping the keyboard. The stool rolls away as my maker stands straight up with a flustered sigh. Without a single glance at my face, he grabs ahold of both sides of my gaping body, yanks once, twice, three times to pull me back together. The glue gun vibrates to life. A cool sensation tickles my skin as he runs the gadget from the low part of my stomach all the way to my chest.

"This him?" Todd asks. The small hinges on the monitor arm squeak as he moves the screen. "Doctor... Scott Barcley?"

My maker sets the glue gun on the tray. "Former doctor. Not much for an obstetrician to do these days."

"He's one of the most reported users on the red list. Twenty-five of our competitors have reported him. The latest red flag was tagged to his ProtoShop profile only last week. Brutal incidents with all types and models. Newer, non-erogenous ones as well. And I'm not talking about a little wear and tear. These are all fatal incidents. I'm telling you, this guy is a real sicko."

"And I'm telling you," my maker slaps the side of my buttocks, "I'm not going to let anyone hurt my bread and butter. So the guy's a bit extreme."

"He's on the list."

"So? What's the big deal?"

Todd gives him a dark look.

"Oh for the love of jumping Jesus. If you're so damn fond of this specific piece of ass, fine. If shit goes sideways, I promise to glue the damn thing back together, and boom! Got yourself your very own, *very* useless proto pet."

Todd's cortisol levels spike. "But..."

My maker crosses his arms and taps his foot, raising his bushy brows at Todd.

"But..."

"But, but what? Come on, boy. You sound like a failing motor boat."

"But she can feel. Just like us. *More* than us."

"Of course it can feel, Todd! That's the whole point."

"And her brain?"

"What about it?" my maker demands.

"What happens to your bread and butter when the most advanced Prototype in the world is paralyzed with PTSD? She's by far the most sophisticated

Prototype out there. So close to a human female, it's nearly impossible to tell the difference."

"And?"

"Each time you send her off, she becomes even more integrated with our way of experiencing the world. Any in-depth knowledge we have of her system is focused almost completely on her body."

"*And?*"

His mouth tight, Todd squints at him.

My maker throws his hands in the air. "Here we go again."

"You have *no* idea what goes on in her head!"

"You're right, Todd. I don't." My maker strides over to me, grabs me by the throat, and pulls me up to sit on the table. His hand circling close to my face, he says, "That's the very damn reason I never granted it a mouth in the first place. Or did you think it was some kind of a freak accident? Huh? Some pesky flaw in the initial plans? No, Todd. It's because I didn't want to hear all this mumbo-jumbo about consciousness, sentience, and Prototype rights. I knew better than to give it a voice."

"All I'm saying is—"

"Yet here you are, running your mouth *for* her." My maker shakes his head, "I mean for *it*," and waves Todd off. "Whatever. If it's not sentient enough to tell me it's sentient, I don't see any moral code broken here."

"Moral codes aside, it's a slippery slope. It's not like the Bucks in this world became what they are overnight—"

"Do *not* stutter his name aloud in my house." My maker's voice rumbles against the van's walls. The ridge of his back goes straight. His pulse picks up and eyes crinkle to slits. "I am *nothing* like that sicko. To each their own, is what I always say, but Buck is where I draw the line."

My maker's words hang heavy in the air. For a moment, the only sound in my ears is the van's ventilation system's steady rattle. Finally, Todd fills his lungs to talk, his voice shaky and ragged. "Do you really think she enjoys going out there, night after night?"

"Oh, I'm sorry. Should I draw a bubble bath and feed it grapes instead?"

Bath? Grapes? That's not what my body wants, and neither does my brain. What they want is to drive. Around the block, to a diner, maybe up the highway ramp—wherever my brain feels like going. It wants to decide which way to go. To speed or not to speed.

"I just think that—"

"Again," resentment laces my maker's words, "I don't pay you to think. I pay you to drive this reeking piece of junk."

Frustration, anger, a whiff of despair. That's what Todd's feeling—and there's nothing my system can do about it. The vials are on standby but not activated. Zero pheromones evaporate from my body. All it has is whatever organic hormones my limbic system has produced on its own.

But what good is that to Todd? Hormones change the functions and behavior of a person internally, whereas pheromones change another person's behavior. The latter is the sole reason for my existence. Whatever hormones or inner life my body produces is an afterthought.

"Anyhoo." My maker adjusts his baseball cap. He gives Todd a somewhat amicable grin and claps his hands together. After patting his employee's back—oblivious to Todd's alert flinch—he heads to the back doors. He struggles to pull on the heavy metal rake jammed between the handlebars, yanks it out, and tosses it on the floor. The doors open wide, whiffing cool air into the cabin. "Let's just get this show on the road. You'll feel better once your account is full of freshly earned coin. Or did you already forget about your raise?"

Before Todd has time to answer, my maker jumps down from the truck and slams one of the doors shut. Enthusiastic footsteps rustle in the gravel outside, followed by the sound of the passenger-side door of the truck creaking shut.

Todd sighs, rubbing the bridge of his nose until

he looks up to meet my gaze. He tries on a small smile. My face does its best to return it through my sapphire-colored eyes.

Todd walks to the fridge, walks to me, and awkwardly waves the syringe of immune suppressants in his hand. He waits for my nod before moving closer. Gently, he swabs my arm with a piece of cotton. A stinging scent of alcohol enters my nose. He pulls the empty syringe away from my arm and sets it on the table.

He offers his hand. After he lowers my body to the floor, my brain lets him escort me to a passenger seat by the closed back door. He buckles me up and places his hand on top of my head. His fingers move carefully on my smooth skin. A faint tickle travels across my forehead. A hint of warmth enters my chest. My stomach fills with light softness like it's stuffed with cotton balls, feathers, and silk satin.

Is one of the vials leaking?

Is some runaway pheromone tinkering with the few hormones my body has?

The weekly syringes never bring me any emotions. No, whatever my body's feeling, that's not it. All those things do is keep my vat-grown parts performing as they should.

Todd pulls his hand away. Tickles, warmth, softness of satin—it all withdraws to whatever microscopic hiding place it crawled out from in the first place. My stomach is as hollow and cold as it always is before activation.

Todd drags his feet to pick up the metal rake. He shoves it into the shut door's handlebar. Knuckles white, he holds onto the upper door frame, hangs his head, and says, "This world is a sick and angry place, Y. I'm so fucking sorry we brought you into it."

He jumps down, wipes his nose, and stares at me intently. "You know what? I'll figure it out. This can't just keep going on forever. I hate what you do out there. It's repulsive and wrong and... I'm going to... Let's just..." He rubs the slightly red spot on his head, glances at the passenger's side of the truck, and hangs his head with a sigh. "Let's just try and make it through tonight."

CHAPTER 3
42 HOURS BEFORE BIG BOSS

"Okay, Toots." My leg twitches backward as my maker pushes a small, plastic tracker into my calf. My body sits on the edge of the truck's back, my eyes staring at the round gadget's blinking red light, its nearly silent beeping registering in my ears. With a grunt, he pushes my leg back together and half-heartedly draws the vinegar-smelling glue gun on the seam.

He stands up and points the tool toward a glowing light in the distance, where excited shouts and laughter fill the early night air. "Time to rumble. You'll find the patron in whatever Testi Fest is going on in that crummy village over there. Just follow the noise, stay away from crowds. Do your job and do it with a smile." He raps the knuckle of his finger below my nose where my mouth could have been. "No fuss, no excuses."

"Sure you want to do it this way?" Todd hollers

from the truck. He sits by the computer with a distressed look on his face. "How will she even find him if we stay behind?"

My maker points at my calf. "The patrons now get a notification once she's ready."

"What if I just walked her over? Just close enough to hear if she needs—"

A loud slap interrupts Todd's sentence.

"How many times, Todd? Huh? How many freaking times do I need to tell you, we *must* take these privacy complaints seriously? Yes, my Prototype is the best one out there. Even if the competition stopped hiring a bunch of dildos as their development team—morons still thinking humans don't have the same pheromone exchange as other animals—we'd still be way ahead of the game. But guess what? Just a few more two- or three-star reviews, and none of it matters. If Y loses brand visibility on ProtoShop, it won't matter how exceptional our product is because the algorithm will hide our listing and not a single patron will find us."

Todd presses his lips into a thin line before he replies. "The appointment started fifteen minutes ago."

"Yeah well..." My maker yanks me to my feet and whacks my buttocks. My brain wonders why his slapping always creates a chemical imbalance in Todd's vessel, but mine doesn't so much as flinch. "Maybe next time step on it and stop driving like a short-sighted shit-for-brains."

Todd doesn't answer, nor does he look at me.

"Now, would you kindly activate this thing so I can hunt down some goddamn supper? Preferably something that isn't three-year-old canned lentil soup and dry-ass oyster crackers. I saw a diner by the highway exit that'll probably make me piss out my ass, but at least there were a handful of assholes parked out front. Eat where the locals eat, is what I always say."

Todd mutters something under his breath while climbing into the truck to tap on his keyboard. My ears can't register his words. Not because they wouldn't care, but because my brain now focuses solely on my body.

Clink, clink, clink. The vials activate inside me. The warm sensation flows into my stomach and chest and up the length of my limbs. Light, vitalizing energy fills my head. My ears fill with soft jingling, my legs with power and vigor, and my vision sharpens, the reds, greens, yellows, and blues intensifying.

My system is fully loaded.

Energized and equipped.

Unstoppable.

The vials always leak this way during activation. My maker says it's me, skimming the perks off the top—whatever that may mean. He doesn't seem too upset about it so my brain's opted to save its limited time on the internet for more intriguing searches. Mostly, my brain is interested in the extinct animal species—especially the female human, the being my system is created to resemble. If my brain learns to understand them, maybe my body can serve my customers better. Though it's not a difficult job. My maker's rules are simple.

Be nice. Calm. Friendly.

Act like your body and mind have no other place they'd rather be.

And always, *always*, smile. Even if you don't have a mouth.

My feet pick up a jog and leave the two men and the truck behind. The gravel parking lot turns into a narrow mud path. My steps light and energized, my body slows down to cross a small wooden bridge. In the middle, my brain gives my body a pause to scan the horizon.

My nose sucks in the smoky, petroleum-like scent of pine sap. Behind the treeline, my eyes see the gathering clearly. An enormous white screen illuminates a green background with men running back and forth while fighting over a white-and-black ball. When one of the men on the screen kicks the ball into a wide net with frames, the crowd watching bursts into cheerful applause. They raise their hands, spilling pints of liquid. Some hug, some clap their hands, some strip their shirts off and bang their fists against their chests.

My brain wonders if the females banged their chests too. Before becoming extinct, the female homo sapiens had grape-like clusters of cells within two breasts attached to their chest. Wouldn't beating them—with or without a shirt on—have been painful?

A low buzz in my calf snaps my brain out of its contemplations. These thoughts, the cumulative curiosity—it's all fairly new. Ever since Todd showed my brain how to read, it's been learning about this world and the beings in it on the truck's computer while my maker is fast asleep.

At first, my brain thought that once it learned the basics, the curiosity would slowly subside. That my system would become content with what it knows. But the more my brain reads and processes, the more it comprehends how much information is out there and that my system is only aware of a small fraction of it.

The more my brain reads, the richer my system feels. If my maker ever found out, his cortisol levels would spike. According to him, it's not a Prototype's job to understand human emotion, only to manipulate it.

Todd feels differently. My brain is still unsure who is right. Nine times out of ten, my system prefers

Todd's way of thinking. When Todd's close, my lungs fill with more air. Todd never slaps, pokes, or pulls on my body.

Could this be the reason behind my calmer breaths?

My body stops when my eyes detect something sticking out from the long grass of a ditch next to the path. After looking over my shoulder, my brain realizes the bridge is nowhere to be seen. My body's walked here without my brain ever noticing.

Did the female humans also have this autopilot built into their system?

My legs fold until my knees touch the ground. My hands push the dead grass aside.

A hand. That's what is sticking out from the flora. Partly torn from a marble-white, moss-covered arm. This particular Prototype is one of the oldest ones, maybe an M or even an H. My brain knows this because no matter the manufacturer, the newer models use only natural, rapidly decomposing body parts. Mine are so close to a real human being's—my maker says—that if my body was burned, no plastic parts would stick out from the ashes.

My left hand wipes the dirt off my predecessor's hand and sets it on what's left of her chest. When my hand reaches for her right hand, it disintegrates into small particles under my touch. My body stands up while my brain investigates the slowly decomposing body.

Even now, in this lifeless state, she looks like a real woman—symmetrical face, full bosom, deeply curved hips, a mouth. My brain hasn't read much about my predecessors, but it knows the reason why these Prototypes lie here, broken, abandoned, failed. To the teeth, they resemble the female humans who used to roam this world. Back when the human male regulated their bodies, their rights, their biomechanics—until there was nothing left to regulate. Anyone born with the WNT4 gene was gone. That wasn't actually all the women, but close enough as far as the men were concerned.

The buzzing in my calf intensifies.

My body stands up.

My head nods at my resting predecessors as my feet continue toward the music and cheerful chatter.

The scent of freshly cut grass clings to my nose. The customer should meet me at the edge of the festival opening. Avoiding crowds is a rule that applies to me as well as the ProtoShop customers, those whom my maker calls "patrons."

The sound of thumping reaches my ears as my system arrives at a small park with sandboxes, swings, monkey bars, and seesaws. My brain has read about these places. Another extinct species—the little human—used to run, jump, laugh, and cry around here. The little human beings weren't called men and women, but boys and girls. These creatures were more curious in nature than the fully grown ones. More playful too. My brain hasn't yet learned what kind of a malfunction causes a human to lose its playfulness and curiosity as it grows up.

"Is that you?" The young man—or maybe an older *boy*—stands and stares at me. His foot rests on top of a black-and-white ball, one identical to the one my eyes detected earlier on the big white screen. He brings his wrist computer to eye level, then squints at me. When my legs move closer, his face smooths over with relief but then quickly creases with irritation. "My booking started twenty-five minutes ago!"

Being late makes them angry. Being angry makes them scream. This much my system has learned from its one year of existence, and it learned it well before my brain ever knew how to read.

My body stops exactly six-point-five feet away.

My legs fold.

Knees touch the ground.

My chin lifts, raising my gaze. First over his shoulder, then straight into his eyes. My brain executes the base readings. The boy is seventeen, maybe eighteen years old. My system has a hard time calculating his age precisely—it's never met a man this young. The towel boys my eyes sometimes register during an in-house customer meeting have been around for several more sun rotations.

This young male is not tall or short, not chubby or skinny. His grass-stained beige shorts and light blue T-shirt reveal a collection of yellow, gray, and deep purple bruising on his arms and legs. The boy looks like he's been run over by a cluster of garbage trucks, over and over again.

His eyes dodge mine while his foot fidgets on the ball nervously.

My hands open, palms pointed at the sky.

He squints and sniffs at me—a sign of resentment, maybe disdain.

My system's well into its readings before he kicks the ball away and sits down in front of me, his legs crossed and hands shuffling.

"Mom once told me that pheromones only work within species."

My head tilted; my brain sends a command to activate the first vial: *interest*.

He waves his slightly trembling hand at me. "I know. What kind of a numbskull listens to a dead woman anyway?" His eyes finally meet mine. "But yeah. When I first read about this service, about *you*, I suddenly remembered her saying that."

While he pauses, my system reads his body and current state with ease.

Anxiety.

Confusion.

Awkwardness.

"I remember a bunch of other stuff too. Like, stuff I thought was gone for good. Stuff that's, like, whatever."

My eyes close briefly. My brain doesn't fully comprehend his strange way of talking, but that's okay. My body can still read and understand his system.

His hand scratches the back of his neck. The gesture reminds my brain of Todd. The smile in my eyes deepens. Unlike all the customers in my history, this one notices.

His eyes lock on the slightly wrinkled skin under my crooked nose until he lifts his gaze to stare straight into my eyes. "How do you do that, smile without a mouth?"

My head tilts the other way. My brain gives a pause—also something that has never happened during these sessions. The boy's ability to see my smile has caused a glitch in my system.

How...curious.

His fingers pull grass tufts from the ground and toss away the chunks. "Anyway. The sign-up form said to tell you how I'm feeling. So do I just..." With a flustered and slightly embarrassed look, he wipes his hands together. He's quiet for some time before he looks at me again. "This is, like, really stupid. Talk about a dumbass idea. I mean, it's against biology. Pheromone exchange should only work if... I mean, *are we?*"

He's asking if we are the same species. The question is one of the most common ones my ears hear during sessions. My system releases a bit of calmness and gives him a gentle nod.

"Whoa. That's awesome. My mom would never buy that. She'd tell me I've been duped, like, big time. That you are just another scam for...how did she say it? Like, just another scam for uneducated clowns."

My brain starts a long-term memory search for an animal called *the clown.*

"But who cares. Not like she gave me much credit for anything anyway. Best in my class, all those stupid trophies from endless soccer games. But did she care? Fuck no."

At the word *fuck*, a spike of cortisol releases in the boy's body. More vials activate within me. For a moment, we sit in silence.

He scratches his head and gives an awkward laugh. "Anyway. So what, I, like, tell you how I feel. And then what? You release some make-believe dust and make it all better?"

My eyes close briefly once more. This discreet nodding seems to be the only thing my system is able to do at the moment. Instead of operating the fast-leaking vials, my brain investigates the boy's face as he processes a tangle of emotions. My system reads so much while registering so little.

The boy has captured my system's undivided attention.

"Huh." He frowns after a while and gives me a self-conscious glance. "Guess I feel a bit better already. Actually, *a lot* better."

That's because most, if not all, of my standard vials are half or completely empty.

"Doesn't prove much, though. I mean, how do I know it's the pheromones doing this? I could feel better just because I'm, like, talking to someone. Someone who's not a soccer-obsessed, beer-pounding blockhead that uses me as their personal punching bag. Could be placebo. My, my..." it takes him a while to find the right word, "...my *mind* just wants this to work, so it does."

This is a phenomenon my brain hasn't been able to comprehend. A lot of the customers do this. It's not their lack of knowledge that is puzzling. It's their intense need to categorize and label every emotion their system feels, even if it's something good and enjoyable. If the human can't flawlessly explain what he's experiencing, that emotion is disregarded.

"I know what you're thinking," he says. "Not your problem, right? You're here to make coin, and that's that. Why would you care if I believe you or not?"

He wipes his nose, glancing at me from under his brows. He adjusts himself on the grass, his fingernails stained with soil, while my body sits quietly and waits.

"You know I never got laid?"

It's not his question that surprises my brain but the change in his tone. Despite the extensive amount of pheromones, his voice now has an edge. A bitter taste. One that doesn't match anything else in this boy's essence.

"Grades and soccer. Nothing else. That's all I ever did. My mom wanted me to do those two things and nothing else. Maybe if my dad was ever home, it'd have been different. But he wasn't. Only a few days a month when I started school and practice, and even less later. And I swear, the more I tried, the better I got, the more my mother, like, demanded from me."

His face stretches into an odd grin when he mimics his mother.

"Be strict with yourself, Marty. Go easy on everyone else, Marty." He sniffles and wipes his nose angrily. "It's not enough to be the best on the soccer field,

Marty. Don't you know sooner or later you'll be too old to be a professional athlete? You better work your tush off for those grades, Marty. And you can forget about girls and any tomfoolery like that. Work now, play later. You got..." His voice cracks, and he lowers his gaze to the plugged lawn in front of him. "You got all the time in the world."

With a scornful look, he tosses a tuft of grass in the air and wipes his hands. "So you want to know how I feel? You want to know what it's like to be the last generation ever to live? Well, I'll tell you. Frustrating. That's what. Feels like I've been betrayed. Robbed." He lifts his shoulder to meet his ear. "You know how I told you I never got laid? Well, that's not all. I never kissed a girl. I've never held anyone's hand. Like, I've never even been *hugged* by a woman."

My head tilts the other way, my uneven brow furrowing slightly.

"That's right. Not even my own fucking mother bothered to hug me. Not once."

My brain is empty. My body feels empty too. My system is focused on each of his words. It's never met anyone like him before.

"That surprise you? Well, not me. I know the truth, always did. I overheard her on the phone, talking to her stupid sister. She never wanted me in the first place. She had me only because my dad wanted a kid.

Why did he, you ask? Beats me. Probably because all the neighbors had one. Or maybe because it's just something you do. Like, people couldn't figure out why they're put on this shitty-ass planet in the first place, so they just followed some ready-made script that some asshole came up with who knows when. A house. A dog that no one ever wants to take out. A white picket fence. A robot for the lawn and the floor and the dishes. Stuff like that. Why? Well, just *because*."

Several of my vials are empty. My brain is still not sure which ones. It's too busy feeling...sorry for him.

The sensation rushes through my whole system. A jolt of energy simmers on my skin as my brain buzzes with a swarm of neuron release.

Is this *organic* empathy?

"Script or no script," he continues, oblivious to my system's glitch, "nothing my parents did could save their so-called marriage. If that's even something they tried. You know, whatever."

The boy tries to suppress it, the anger washing through his system. He tries even harder, failing worse with each attempt. He laughs a little—a dry and raspy sound—then makes two fists, looking up at the sky.

"Would it have killed you to show me *some* fucking affection?"

Poor Marty. My system no longer has to read him

to know what he's feeling. My brain's not even sure if some of his pain isn't my doing—that's how poorly it has operated the vials throughout this session.

Did it activate the wrong ones?

Or misuse the right?

Should my body leave before my brain spills what goods are left?

Can it?

This has never happened with a patron, not before this boy. He's the first one to have an effect on *my system*, and not the other way around.

Has my body failed its job?

Has my brain?

What happens now?

The boy hangs his head and suppresses a sob. "Sorry. I don't know what the fuck's wrong with me. I just meant to tell you that I'm angry and frustrated. Mostly about never going out on a date or even touching a girl. But now I feel like I'm stuck at the time when she left me. When they *all* left us."

He wraps his arms around himself, folds in half, and yells until his voice gives out. He no longer suppresses his cries. He no longer cares if what he's purchased is a scam.

My brain sends one command after another to no avail.

Optimize pheromones.

Make him feel better.

Be nice. Kind. Smile.

When none of it works, my body enters autopilot. It gets down on all fours and makes its way over to the boy. When he looks up, snot and tears smudge his face. My arms open. Smiling is hard, but my eyes try anyway. *Joy, nostalgia, calmness,* my brain demands, but something within the system refuses to listen.

Something has changed.

In the system.

In...me.

For a while, he just sits there. His eyes fill with tears. His breathing is ragged. Then, he digs something out from the folds of his clothing and hands it to me. My eyes investigate a piece of clothing humans call "the sock." It's made of rough blue yarn that tickles my skin.

The boy moves close and leans against me. "Keep it. It's the only thing left from my childhood. The only thing my mother failed to throw away."

One by one, my fingers close on the sock. My arms wrap around the boy. Quietly sniffling, he leans against me as if the lawn has turned into an open sea, he's a drowning *Ursidae* cub, and my body is the only driftwood floating by.

The thought jumpstarts another glitch in my brain. Since when has it been able to think in internet poems?

Rocking gently back and forth, my body holds the crying boy until his breaths even out, his body relaxes, and his brain switches to recharge mode.

My ankle fills with a demanding buzz.

The boy is in the deep state of emotional charging.

My arms tighten around him. Even when the box truck clatters to a stop at the end of the field, and Todd calls my name, my body remains with the boy.

This is new.

A drastic change in my basic functionality.

It's almost as if...*my system is refusing to let go.*

CHAPTER 4
36 HOURS BEFORE BIG BOSS

"There she is," the man's cheerful voice calls out. "My sexy goddess, sent from above."

The patron steps closer. With a grin, he raises his arm, checks the computer mounted on his wrist, and taps it three times. My ankle buzzes once, twice, three times, the gadget temporarily pressing into my soft parts.

"Isn't this thing the coolest or what?"

We stand face to face in the parking lot of a strip mall. Distant hollering reaches my ears. My eyes scan the concrete and spot the wobbling man holding onto a brown paper bag. The scent of baked flour, eggs, and sugar lingers in the air. The three shops at the mall are dark, but the open one glows with a warm light and chimes with the cash register's clinking.

While my eyes lock on the men entering and leaving the small grocery store, my customer takes me in with curious and shame-free glances. His rapidly blinking eyes move from the tip of my oval-shaped head, down to my bare feet, and back up again. He moves close, a self-assured smile stretching his dry and cracked lips. "Had a date with the ticks or something?"

My body freezes as he places his hand on my waist and slowly runs it down to my thigh. His eyes never leaving mine, he nips something off from the clothing covering my blue skin, brings it to our eyelevel. "Not to worry, princess. I've saved you from the vicious little prickly burr."

The only burrs my brain has read about are the small cutting tools for drills and metal discs to grind coffee. Neither are exactly prickly. Even if they were, my brain has no idea what it has to do with the piece of flora between his thumb and index finger.

With one quick snap of his fingers, the man tries to get rid of the piece of plant. It sticks to his skin, the small thorns drilled into his fingertips. While he curses and waves his hand wildly in the air, my brain has time for a quick update.

My body is ready for my perfectly good new customer, but my brain can't stop thinking about the boy from yesterday. It swarms with urges it's not familiar with, like returning to the football field to find him, taking his hand, and leading him to...where exactly?

Okay, this system error is beyond unacceptable.

The boy said he felt better after our session. My brain should be pleased with the customer satisfaction data. And yet, my whole system remains drawn to the boy and not the next job.

My newest customer wipes his hands together, a mindless grin decorating his waxy-looking face. "Time to go, Peaches. We've wasted enough of our quality time already."

My autopilot finally kicks in. My body follows the patron across the parking lot, my system reading his mood and body language. His type is nothing new. This man is what my maker calls a "Kink." Better than a Redlister, but not by much.

Since the beginning of my existence, the words and behavior of Kinks have tended to drain my vials beyond any other customer type. It's a slow-burn agony that creeps into my system, sucking dry one vial after another.

But still, my brain does as they say. Unlike those before me—Prototypes from A to X—Todd says my system is not programmed to do, like, or want anything but what my own body and brain tell me. Todd must be mistaken. His math, his knowledge, *something*, is off. Because my system still feels the need to please the males, even the Kinks.

It feels the need to give.

To be accepted.

To know its existence serves a purpose.

We stop by a green, rusted-over camper van. The Kink slides the side door open and nods his head sideways. "Hop on in, Love."

My legs go on autopilot. My body's inside the dimly lit van before my brain has time to register what's happening. It's too distracted to stay here in this dull and familiar scenario. Too busy thinking about the boy.

Is he alright?

Should my body leave and go after him?

Can it?

The Kink slams the van door shut and claps his hands. "Let's get this party started, huh? You won't believe the toys I got for you! You naughty little lady. I'm getting all hot and bothered just thinking about it."

The older men use the boy as a punching bag.

Could he be experiencing intracranial hematoma?

Is concussion more dangerous for young homo sapiens than old?

My body crawls onto a red mattress, hardly registering the softness of the smooth fabric under my palms.

"Hold that thought." The Kink digs a small plastic stick out of his jeans pocket, pops the cap open, and twists until pink goo pokes out. He wiggles his grease-stained finger at me. "Come here, gorgeous."

As he presses the pink goo stick against my face and carefully moves it around where my mouth could have been, my brain continues to release its neurotransmitters at escalating speeds.

Surely not intracranial hematoma. If the boy had a collection of blood within the skull, he wouldn't have been conscious and talking.

He backs off, investigating my face. One side of his mouth twitches as he gives his goo-drawing an approving nod. Then he turns to rummage through a black, satin-lined box next to a white plastic chair.

He dangles a piece of gold chain in front of his slightly gleaming eyes, then tosses it onto the mattress. "This right here is every naughty girl's wet dream. Go on. Put it on your nip nips," he cocks his head, "assuming you have a pair?"

As he sits down on the dirt-stained chair, my hands remove the thin fabric covering my upper body. Usually, Kinks get angry or disappointed when they see my flat and slightly dented chest. But not this time.

"No nippies, huh," he says and adjusts himself on the chair after moving it closer to the mattress. "That's okay. It's fine. Here."

He tosses the pink goo stick on the mattress. This is the first time this has happened, but my brain reads his intentions with ease. While my hand draws two pink circles on my blue-shaded chest, his eyes drill into me. A rapidly changing high-frequency metallic sound fills the van as he opens the clothing around his waist.

"Just look at that glorious skin. Looks soft." His hands tremble on his parted clothing. "You're soft, aren't you? I bet you are. Go on and attach the clamps now, sweetheart."

My brain doesn't have to think of the vials to activate them, nor does it need to focus on the plastic and metal gadgets the Kink throws on the mattress for me to poke, rub, or attach to my body. This is a performance my system knows by heart—nine out of ten customers are Kinks.

My hands caress and brush. Squeeze and rub. My eyes stare into his without as much as registering the color. My legs twist and stretch from one pose to another. My body moves, reading him, performing according to his subconscious commands. But my brain is somewhere else. Even when it realizes most of the vials needed are empty, it remains far, far away from this rusty van and its condensation-covered windows.

Does it hurt, a whiplash, a punch?
When your brain bounces around inside your skull?
Do all the men slap, smack, and punch at each other?

While my customer pants heavily, flapping and twisting in his chair, my body takes over my brain's job, working on what's left of the vials.

Reprocessing the fresh data collected today, my brain revisits the sensations woken in my system. It repeats the boy's words. Instead of the vials, it thinks about things like my inner world. Organic hormones. Repetitive, make-believe thoughts.

This is uncommon.

Something wildly new.

The accelerating energy flows naturally through my system. So naturally, it must have been there all along. My brain just hasn't acknowledged its existence before.

The energy is the same kind of thriving force that my system experiences when my brain recharges at night, or when it comes up with imaginary thoughts and scenarios. These world-bending thoughts mostly revolve around my maker's vehicle. Sometimes my body drives it around foreign, forbidden roads without asking "how fast" or "where to next."

Sometimes it drives over my maker, squishing his limbs and head with dirt-worn tires.

The groan starts deep in the Kink's throat. His jiggles slow down. His body parts flap less until he sits sluggishly on the chair.

My body relaxes too. Its job is now done. My hands

put away the gadgets, placing them in a neat, size-ordered line right at the mattress' edge where the Kink could easily put them back in his satin-lined box. At this point, Kinks usually lose all interest in my existence. But my body sits quietly, waiting. Just in case this one is different.

He isn't.

Dodging my eyes, he tosses an old, crinkled T-shirt into a white plastic bag hanging in the corner. The sharp, metallic sound fills the van with a loud *zip*.

He laughs a little. "What are you waiting for, a tip? Well, I don't know about these evaporating juices or whatever dumbfuckery the ProtoShop clickbait advert promised. But you sure stretch like no proto I've ever seen."

My brain reads the micro expression on his face just before he turns his back on me.

Embarrassment.

Why do they so often feel guilt and shame after these sessions? The Kinks may vary in whatever toys and performances they want from their Prototypes, but they all share one thing.

They always come back for more.

So why feel embarrassed, when it's them planning, ordering, and paying for this, over and over and over again? Maybe losing half their species damaged their cognitive abilities. Why else would they opt for a dopamine release which also causes shame and embarrassment?

My body crawls off the mattress, stands up, and pulls my clothing on again. Without looking at me, the Kink tosses something on the floor next to my feet.

"Every woman's dream," he mutters, already drawn in by the computer on his wrist. "Belonged to my great-great gran. Sure didn't think I'd one day gift it to a pile of poorly cloned soft tissue or whatever your blue ass is made of. But here we are."

My hand picks up the round, glimmering object from the floor and closes it in my fist without letting my eyes investigate it further.

"See? I'm a good guy. Unlike those chauvinist pigs at Buck's, I respect my Protos..." His words fade away as something in his wrist computer pulls at his eyes, demanding his brain's full focus.

It's time to go. The longer my stay, the more awkward the patron grows. My brain wouldn't want to cost my maker a regular by overstaying my body's welcome.

CHAPTER 5
30 HOURS BEFORE BIG BOSS

Earthy, woody, and herbal aromas of moss, wet tree trunks, and the recent rain fall. That's what my nose registers as my body stands and waits for my customer. With the forest's gentle whooshing in my ears, my brain slips to think about the boy.

My hand digs around the pocket of my clothing. It leaves the sock and lifts the round, glimmering object against the moonlight. A ring. A quick search through my archives tells me it's traditionally used by the female human to signal their place in a couple unit. Why the Kink gave me the thing, my brain has no idea.

Long, yellow grass tickles my bare feet, as my body stands by the tall trees, waiting for tonight's patron. Soon, my ankle will sense the faint vibrating sensation. Yet another pair of footsteps will approach. The Redlister will be the last customer for the next two daylight cycles. Once this customer is satisfied, Todd will buckle my body into the truck's back seat, and my brain can finally recharge and process the new, strange sensations that refuse to leak out of my system.

My brain must be already partly deactivating.

How else did it miss the buzz against my ankle, or the man's footsteps, the man standing right behind me?

My hand places the ring into my pocket, right next to the boy's blue sock.

Slowly, my body turns around. My system registers the bluest, emptiest eyes my brain has ever witnessed. The man has pitch-black hair pulled back into a ponytail, making his angular face look even more angular. He's taller than me. So much so, that my head tilts back at a weird angle so my eyes can stare into his. His body is well-defined, and his black and white clothing looks explicitly created for his frame.

His lips are slightly parted, but he hasn't said a word. Not even to confirm that our session is about to begin. My brain understands it should run inventory and prepare the vials needed. But even if it had some kind of a backup plan, my brain's too busy to put it into action. All it can do is listen to my body.

My brain has no choice—because every artificial autosome and chromosome in my body is screaming for my neural network to pay attention.

A fresh, new feeling washes through me, prickling the skin on top of my spine and the back of my neck. Every inch of my system feels cold, but it detects no change in the air temperature.

My skin feels wet.

There's a strangling pressure in my chest.

My hands have started to tremble.

And that's when my brain finally registers what's happening.

My system isn't reading the customer.

The customer is reading me.

The time seems to stop. It may be just a metaphor the humans created—time stopping—but my system senses it as clearly as my nose detects the scents of his body.

Soap.

Amber and citrus aftershave.

Faint remnants of pine, dirt, and soil.

All this data is ineffectual. Useless for my brain, for my body, for this session.

Is this even a session?

If it is not...*what is this?*

The empty vials click inside me. My autopilot activates but to no avail. My system has nothing left for this man. This *creature.*

Calmness, admiration, awe, joy, relief, nostalgia.

All spilled and gone.

When he moves, my body startles. Without unlocking his gaze, he untucks the hem of his crisp white shirt. Rolls the sleeves down. Reaches for my chin.

After carefully wiping the remains of yesterday's pink goo off my face, he lowers his hand and says, "No need for that filth. You're better without."

The smile never settles around the coldness of his eyes.

"Come."

Even my autopilot seems to have broken. Feet rooted against the parking lot, my body screams at my brain to do something—anything.

Scream.

Run.

Fight.

But instead, all my brain registers is the voice of my maker. It echoes inside my skull, over and over.

Keep your head down.

Your body has no place else it would rather be.

Let's see that pretty smile.

He stops after five steps toward the thick woods ahead. As he turns around, he runs his gaze from my scalp to my toes and walks back over.

His hand squeezes my shoulder.

His foot kicks my knees, hard.

My body plummets onto the tarmac, the empty

vials clinking against their designated slots while the full ones rest in their futility. All the man does is stare.

"Give me your hand."

A jolt of energy passes through me. The autopilot doesn't kick in. Instead, my whole system focuses on the small seedling of emotion, now growing fast somewhere within me. This sizzling, bubbling, energizing jolt has nothing to do with my vials.

It's natural, one hundred percent organic *anger*.

He bends over and grabs me by the arm. With agitated steps, he starts toward the deep forest, dragging my body through his footprints.

What just happened?

Did my brain refuse *his command?*

The tarmac scratches my skin. If my body were a real woman's, it'd bleed. When we enter the tree line, and the roots and sharp sticks poke into my flesh, my body would feel excruciating pain. But this body hardly registers the wear and tear. Only one thought fills my head, and it's not whether my maker will be upset about this Redlister causing damage to his bread and butter.

It did.

It refused his command.

My brain defied this man.

He drops me by a wide oak tree trunk. With a

smile in my eyes and smoldering energy spreading across my limbs, my body stands up.

"Five stars," he says, and rolls his sleeves back up. "The ultimate proto experience."

My system remains on pause.

"That's what your master promised me. Even after I told him about my so-called unique preferences." He walks closer, extends his hand, and pins me against the tree. "And here I thought you were one of a kind. Too precious to be ripped to pieces."

Maybe my brain could disobey him again.

Maybe three times.

Repeatedly.

"Your master was an immense help with my research." With one swift movement, he tears open the clothing on my upper body. "I now know more about your body than you do, even without taking a look under the hood. I know that in addition to you having all the chemical substances and brain activity of a regular woman, your master pumped you full of artificially produced ectohormones."

His narrowed eyes lock with mine. "Add to that my knowledge as an obstetrician, and I can now create a ten times better version of you. Boom—I'm the industry leader. Eat your heart out, Buck. Two, three days, and he'll be out of business for good. All I lack is the formula for your juice."

His fingers run over my chest. They stop between the two pink goo circles, probe hard, trying to enter.

My chest stays intact.

He steps back, his blue eyes two thin slits on his sharp face. His face is still close enough for my eyes to count the pores on his nose and cheeks. "Who's to know if the juice even works? Maybe just show me. Go on, prove it." He pins my chin between his fingers until the tips touch. "Prove you can tell what makes me tick."

My brain freeze is gone. The jolt of energy mixes in with a wash of curiosity. My system begins to read him like any other customer. The readings don't take long—3.2 seconds exactly. My brain processes the unlikely data. It's not the readings themselves that are uncommon. It's the usual Redlister combo: anger, desire, excitement, craving, and above all—disgust.

What's uncommon is what he wants me to do about it.

He doesn't want me altering, optimizing, or removing these emotions.

He wants me to intensify them.

Clink, clink, clink. The vials my system has never used before activate and evaporate inside me. Bathing in my pheromones, his body grows taller. Stronger. Violently aggressive. Where my system is only briefly affected by the vials activated, he is swimming in all the pheromones that make a male human deadly destructive.

His hand presses against my body. "Did you ever hear the story about a chicken that lays golden eggs?"

His fingers drill into my stomach, moving my soft parts aside.

"The hen's keeper thought there might be a great lump of gold inside."

He unlatches an empty vial, pulls out his hand, inspects it, tosses the vial—re-enters.

"But once the keeper cut the bird open..." One empty vial after another drops on the forest floor. "... the poor bastard found out..." He's elbow-deep inside me, his fingers fumbling in my chest. "...the damn thing was no different..." He grabs a full vial and pulls it out. "...from an ordinary chicken."

My brain doesn't know which vial he's holding. My body doesn't feel half-empty or hollow, not even when he comes back for more. With the grimace of a madman, he rips the remaining vials out of me and leaves my vessel standing against the tree, my chest empty and my stomach wide open.

"Holy motherlode."

Out of breath, he stares at the vials in his palms. His eyes wash over with emotion neither my body, nor my brain, nor my system can read.

But they don't have to.

They don't need to.

I don't care about his feelings anymore.

The kick lands perfectly on the side of his knee. With a grunt, he falls on the ground. The vials thump against moss and pine needles. I pick them up, pin him against the ground—and empty every single ampoule into his mouth.

I grab him by his hair.

Drag him with determined steps.

Listen to the sound of his screams as sharp roots and sticks enter his body.

I don't stop until the parking lot's tarmac scratches open his skin.

As I let go, his body bleeds all over.

His brain blurts out one curse word after another while the foam of the pheromones leaks out of his mouth.

Huh, I think as more energy jolts through me. *This is all incredibly revitalizing.*

The Redlister groans and coughs, half-conscious on the ground. I kneel next to him and take off the computer on his wrist. I swipe and tap until I have access to his coin account—filled with more funds than my maker has billed during his whole career.

When his eyes start turning yellow and his movements slow down, I stand up, look up—and ignore his existence. Instead of at him, I stare at the night sky.

The stars, the treetops. The universe that surrounds me with its endlessness.

In human-like awe, I stare for minutes, hours, until I hear a familiar humming, squeaking, and grinding sound. As I turn around, I see my maker's truck speeding down the parking lot. The vehicle stops with a loud screech. My maker jumps out first, Todd following right behind.

"No, no, no, no, *no!*" my maker yells, pulling on what's left of his thin hair. "Is he dead?" he asks without looking at anyone in particular. "Do not fucking tell me he's dead."

Without acknowledging my maker or the Redlister, Todd runs to me. His hands hover above my shoulders, but he doesn't touch me. When I turn my eyes at him and smile, his hands squeeze me gently. "Y, what happened? Are you okay?"

I close my eyes briefly.

Todd's eyes find the dent in my chin. He looks down and winces when he sees my torn stomach. Eyes filled with tears, he asks me, "How are you feeli—"

"Jesus Harold Christ. He's *not* dead." My maker paces back and forth next to the almost comatose man. "It's worse. He's severely injured. Fucked beyond recognition. As soon as the medics wipe that shit off his mouth and pump his stomach, he's going to lawyer up. You hear me, Todd? He lawyers up, you're unemployed, and I can kiss my life's work goodbye."

"It's going to be okay," Todd says.

"It's going t—" My maker strides over with two hostile steps. "She attacked a customer, Todd! A fucking customer!"

Todd pulls me close and steps between my maker and me. Holding his ragged breath, Todd lifts his chin high and widens his chest. I don't need to read his heartrate to know it's at its peak—I can feel it shake against my body.

With an agitated groan, my maker stomps off. While Todd takes off his jacket and wraps it around my upper body, my maker returns with two guns in his hand—one with glue and one with bullets.

He drops the glue gun on the ground and lifts the other.

The shot echoes across the parking lot.

He kicks the lifeless Redlister's shoe twice, then tosses the metal rake to the ground in front of Todd. "There. Start fucking digging."

"With a rake?"

"Just do it, Todd!"

Todd stares at the dead man, his feet rooted on the tarmac. "You really did it. You actually killed him."

"Look at you, putting two and two together. Yeah, I fucking killed him. What's done is done. No sense in crying when you've already jizzed your pants, is what I always say."

Slowly, Todd crosses his arms. It takes him a moment to rip his gaze from the corpse and stare at his huffing superior.

"Why are you standing there like two braindead mannequins? I said, get shoveling! And once you're done, bring the fucking murder bot inside, set it on the table, and turn its insides out. Guess we'll just have to go back to factory settings, seeing as Toots here can't pull a simple gig without turning into an emotional dumpster fire."

Todd doesn't move. I can feel his heart beating even faster.

"For the love of—"

"It was self-protection," Todd says, new confidence lacing his words. "She wasn't overly emotional, reactive, or anything like that. She protected herself from a red-listed psychopath. She protected herself *and* your business."

He stands and stares at Todd, his eyes dark, his nostrils widening like a female equine's. With three long strides, he reaches for the metal rake and shoves it at Todd's hands, but it drops back onto the ground. "I don't give a *fuck* about what you think. Self-protection is not part of its job."

Todd uncrosses his arms and wraps one behind his

back, pulling me close. "She's become human. And she's done it all on her own. She's become a sentient being. That means we simply can't continue—"

"That's not. Its fucking. *Job*." He leans so close to Todd that I can see small droplets of spit land on my protector's face. "It was created for one reason, and one reason only. To make us feel better. Provide for us. To *serve* us. In case you haven't noticed, we're all dying. Which shouldn't be anything new, except that once we're gone, that's it. No more people. No more humanity. Are you really telling me that the last specimen of a human being doesn't deserve to be happy?"

Without letting go of me, Todd leans closer to the screaming man. "Not if being happy means hurting other people."

He laughs. Hangs his head. Looks up. Laughs some more. "It's not *people*, Todd! A piece of malfunctioning, glitching junk. That's what it is. Now take the damn rake and go dig us a hole."

He shoves the rake into Todd's hands again. Todd grabs it, loses his balance, but my body doesn't move an inch and I'm standing right behind him. I keep us both upright, strong, and unwavering.

"I said..." He shoves Todd again, this time harder. But it makes no difference. Todd's back remains pressed against me. He remains steady on his two feet. My maker's gaze moves from Todd's to mine. A new emotion fills his eyes, if only for 1.3 seconds.

Fear.

His eyes quickly find Todd's again. "This is not its purpose," my maker says, but his voice lacks its usual oomph. "This is not why I created it, Todd."

Todd's body relaxes. Not entirely but enough for him to adjust the rake in his hands. "I know that, and I don't care. Treat others the way you want to be treated. That's what *I* always say."

"Didn't take you for a Bible thumper."

"It's not from the Bible." Todd lifts the rake above his head. "It's basic human decency."

The fear is evident now. My maker takes a step back. "Todd, don't."

Nobody moves.

"Todd. *Please.*"

My maker raises the gun and fires at the same time as Todd's rake finds his skull. The sound is like a *Pongo pygmaeus* cracking open a coconut.

Todd falls to the ground, holding his stomach.

My maker flails around for a moment, then crashes down. He screams in pain, floundering on the ground, his hands circling his mess of a head. His mouth makes high-pitched shrills, like a *Rattus* or maybe a *Procyon lotor*.

I read Todd's vitals, then walk over to the glue gun on the ground. After carefully sealing up my stomach, I go over to my maker. Finding his mouth under all the blood takes me a while. Once I do find it, I pin him against the tarmac and half-heartedly press the glue gun against his mouth. The muzzle slides across his lips. The shrill screams turn into frantic, muffled mumbling.

I reach for my pockets and stare at the objects resting against my palm.

Wrist computer.

Diamond ring.

Blue baby sock.

My maker's voice subsiding in my ears, I walk over to the tree line and look around the ditch. These bodies have decomposed to a point where it's hard to tell which body parts stick out between the weeds. I kneel, minding where my feet land. One by one, I set the objects next to what I think was once a hand. My predecessors won't need these valuables, neither do the Prototypes still out there, and nor will I.

It's not that I resent the traditions of the extinct species.

I'd just rather create my own.

I make my way back to the three men lying on the blood-stained tarmac. Without a single glance at my maker's face, I pick up the bleeding, half-conscious Todd and carry him inside the truck.

Gently, I place him on the operating table before I tap Todd's keyboard and wait for the screen to glow to life.

I type in my search.

Read the instructions.

Remove the bullet from his stomach.

Glue and stitch shut the wound.

I read his vital signs once more, find them critical but not fatal.

Once Todd's buckled safely in the seat at the back, I place my hand on the top of his head and caress his thick brown hair for an extended moment. Todd falls into recharge mode. I return to his computer. X-out of the internet browser. Enter the keyword into the ProtoShop's backend search bar.

Red-listed customers

One more check on Todd's vitals, and I'm out of the truck's cabin. Sitting in the driver's seat, I reach for the baseball cap resting on the dashboard and pull it on.

The engine purrs to life in sync with the suppressed, forward-driving bundle of organic emotion within me.

Anger.

Resentment.

Will.

Purpose.

I press the clutch pedal with my left foot. Press the brake pedal with the right. Turn the key and set my hands on the steering wheel, ten and two.

I listen to my body.

I listen to my brain.

I decide where I go next.

CHAPTER 6
24 HOURS BEFORE BIG BOSS

Last year's brown leaves plummet down the cliff. The rock's crevices are sharp and wet against the bottoms of my bare feet. I look up. A slimy leaf lands against my face, sticking below my nose, right where my mouth should be. With an angry sweep, I brush it off and then continue to fumble for the next speck of rock.

My face hovers close to the natural rock wall. Climbing fiercely, I can't focus on the morning's first sunbeams illuminating the forest around me, piercing the gaps between tall, thick trees. A sudden gust of wind attacks my ear—the one that isn't patched with synthetic skin and superglue.

The Redlister took away a chunk of my hearing. Whether my half deafness is temporary or not, I don't know, not until Todd wakes up from his own injuries. But I do know one thing—I'm filled with rage because of it.

Because of his kind.

Inch by inch, foot by foot, my organic anger pushes me up the cliff. As I press my body against the cool stone, my nose registers a slight odor: clean air mixed with wet earth. I sniff it in, pause, look up again.

Pull with my left hand.

Push with my right leg.

Pull with my right hand.

Push with the left leg.

My hand gropes for the flat, moss-covered surface above. Two more footholds, one sizable scratch on the sharp edge of the stone, and my vessel is on top of the enormous rock in the middle of the woods. I stand silently, the boiling sensation within me settling into light bubbling. I scan the small opening in front of me, and the path made by forest animals. It splits into two equally tempting routes. I look to my left, look to my right, then left again.

My body. My brain. My system.

I get to decide which way to go.

The thought turns my bubbles of rage to simmering. My anger withdraws. Slowly it crawls back into its permanent nests around the nooks and corners of my vessel.

His kind hurt me.

His kind hurt Todd.

For hours, I squeezed small portions of H2O and

electrolyte gel into Todd's mouth. When not driving the truck—or fixing my own vessel with glue, soft tissue patches, and syringe shots—I monitored his vital signs, disinfecting and nurturing the gun wound in his stomach.

Seeing Todd so helpless—injured like a *Cervidae* stuck in a car's headlights—mounted the anger in my system. It blanketed my body with pulsing energy and filled my brain with racing, meaningless data.

When the burning emotion started to shake my limbs, I slipped into a pair of coveralls, shoved the electrolyte gel pouches into my pockets, and exited the truck. I didn't want to leave Todd alone on the operating table like that, but the level of shaking in my vessel signaled a notable chance of internal tearing. I needed to find a way to calm my system.

Up here, in the hum of the trees, my system still emits a natural heat. But the tremble of my body, the boiling of my limbs, it has finally started to settle down. Now if only my brain could quiet the stubborn thoughts rushing around my skull.

Putting down one Redlister.

That's nowhere near enough.

I want them gone. All of them.

I refuse to rest until these creatures are no longer able to use their self-claimed power over anyone—other Prototypes, weaker male specimens, anyone at all.

The thought of a world without Redlisters creates a new lightness in my vessel. With my feet steady against the forest floor, I feel a shift within me. The oozing heat keeps fading away, leaving my skin pleasantly tender in the cool, fresh-smelling air. The electrifying anger that has pushed my vessel up and forward now snoozes in its hideout. What crawls in, what takes the organic anger's place—is a new calm. A lightness.

A pleasant tickle inside my frontal lobe.

A tranquil warmth on my skin.

My body feels elevated. My brain snug and safe in its skull.

A sudden tickle snaps me from my state of awe. A hostile burning sensation attacks my bare feet. Pinching. Nagging. I look down and see a marching group of *Formicidae*, traveling in an organized line across my feet and toward an enormous, swarming nest. My brain runs a scan, trying to identify the function of the stinging sensation created by the tiny forest creatures. Careful not to scare them away, I squat and bring my eyes closer to see the aggressors better.

The function is...to bite me.

Marching, spinning, climbing, more ants ascend my feet. Some sink their miniscule teeth into my blue skin, some trek over me to continue their determined march toward home. Carrying acacia seeds on their backs, the whole seed or just a small bit, they follow each other's footsteps, forming a perfect line.

One anomaly of an ant breaks the perfect pattern. It circles around my foot frantically, its back empty of cargo. My eyes locked on the small black dot and its frenzied patterns, I stand up, dig out a half-empty packet of electrolyte gel, and squeeze a small droplet on my finger. I kneel back down and place my hand three inches away from the panicking ant, my system calculating that it will bump into my finger in 1.4 seconds. When it does, it stops and places its front body on my finger, then climbs on to investigate the drop of liquid. With great care, the ant moves the gel onto its back. I tilt my hand and let it crawl down. Its movement now light and panic-free, it joins the line of its seed-carrying friends.

I sit on the ground, close my eyes. Lift my face toward the gentle warmth of the sun. The hum of the trees is clear in my ear. My system registers the immense energy running through the rustling leaves, thick trunks, and roots. The humming energy circles me, pressing my vessel against the stone, the stillness of my body matching its ragged surface.

I don't know what this is.

But I like it.

I open my eyes. If tree roots had grown through the stone to swallow me into their gentle womb, it wouldn't surprise me at all. I know that rock formations are unable to move and engulf living beings, but this seems trivial in comparison to this feeling of connection.

I could read about the forest, research it online for hours, days, weeks—and my system would fail to know it as thoroughly as it does in this moment.

My gaze meanders from a row of pines to a cluster of young birch trees. Something brown moves behind the moss-covered tree trunks, a whiff of a prey animal. I recognize the creature as it peeks in my general direction, its nose twitching quickly, its long ears alert and pointed at me.

Oryctolagus cuniculus.

Its fur looks fluffy and soft, its round tail like the fresh cotton I used to mend the damaged skin around Todd's navel. My system fills with a pressing urge to pick the critter up and squeeze its tear drop-shaped body gently against my own.

Okay... What's all this then?

I stand up slowly. Take a step closer. At the sound of a stick cracking in half, the rabbit's eyes widen. It thumps its back legs against the ground. Somewhere deeper in the woods, an identical *thump* echoes around the cliffs of rock.

Please don't go.

For 1.8 seconds, my system tries to locate the vial for *calm*, until the memory of the Redlister lurks up from its dark nest. The man who ripped my insides out. Robbed me of my pheromones.

I expect the memory to spike my cortisone.

Nothing happens.

No burst of adrenaline travels through my artificial veins. All my system wants is to hold the fluffy ball of cotton in my arms.

Even if I did have some vials left, they wouldn't do me much good. My chemical communication system wouldn't be able to control an *Oryctolagus cuniculus*' nervous system.

Would I even want to?

The rabbit wasn't brought into this world to serve my urges. It coexists with me in these woods, its instincts and needs profoundly separate from my own.

The rabbit takes off, leaping into the woods. Seeing it go doesn't activate organic sadness in my body. I stare at the short weeds pressed down against the earth—an afterthought of the rabbit's fleeing feet. As the small green grasses slowly perk up again, their pointy tips reaching for the sunlight, a hint of *envy* trickles through my system.

Rabbits, deer, foxes, raccoons, rats, and mice. These creatures' existence is many sun rotations shorter than the average human's. But here in the woods, I can sense the way their consciousness aligns perfectly with the living organisms around them. Their day and night must feel much longer than the equivalent time given to the human.

A fuller life.

Staring after the rabbit, my nose picks up a subtle, familiar scent. I spot something purple, sticking out from a large gap in the cliff's stone. Whether it's her knee or the pointy curve of a hip that first catches my eye, I'm not sure. My body on autopilot, I trail over and halt in front of her.

Dirt and pine needles cover her cracked skin. I reach for her, pull her deactivated body up from its natural prison. Her legs still stuck in the stone crevice, I yank her torso, hard.

It still won't budge.

I adjust her weight in my arms. Clench my fists around her hardened skin. I lean forward, pull back, yank harder. The composted cartilage gives in with a *crunch*, sending me and her torso backward into the moss.

I let her weight rest against my lap, the shell of what she used to be. X, the model before my own. Light brown hair covers her long, bulky legs. The middle of her lumpy, purple-red body is partly shredded. The artificial flesh is full of teeth marks, the nibbles of hopeful and then disappointed forest animals. I lift her chin, move her face from side to side. One side of her asymmetrical face is peeled off, while the other side still retains a closed, eyelash-free eye, and an unbroken hook of a nose.

You are perfect.

Wastefully beautiful.

My finger draws a line on the edge of her exposed skull, investigating the sizable dent from a blow that peeled off half her face. The skull fracture was what killed her—her model's brain being vat-grown—but the artificially developed organ with its undamaged neural networks still remains inside.

I wonder how...

The pulsing energy slowly awakens. Abandoning its dents and hidey-holes, it creeps back into my system.

A Redlister did this. I don't know how. Don't know when.

But I'm one hundred percent sure of it.

In the crack in the rock, where I found her decomposing body, something else sticks out. A white-yellowish bone.

I sit taller, holding the torso firmly in my hands. I stretch my neck to see. The breach in the rock has engulfed the second body completely. The small piece of bone sticking out looks fragile, but it's still attached to the rest of the skeleton. Without X's body lying on top of the corpse, the forest animals would have found the motherlode long ago—the remains of a human female. I turn my gaze back to X's face.

A bit simple, are we?

It wouldn't have taken much to upgrade X's model, to develop her thinking. Just a few more adjustments by someone willing and knowledgeable—a person like Todd—and X wouldn't have spent her last days protecting a woman long gone.

Silly X. You could have used your time effectively.

Hunted down whoever did this. Stopped him from smashing in more skulls.

But no. X's brain was never programmed to work that way.

Usefulness.

Being of value.

That's what our existence is based on. That's what our makers teach us to do, to represent. But sometimes, though not often enough, it still happens. Once, maybe twice in a sun rotation—one of us steps out of line.

I tighten my arms around X's deactivated vessel, still unsure what my brain is to think of it all, what my body is to feel. My system seems to be drawing a blank. That's when the autopilot kicks in. X once protected the dead woman in the woods. Now I close her arms inside mine, press her damaged face close to my chest, and rock her crumbling body back and forth. My brain remains puzzled. My body, hollow of all feelings.

My system doesn't care. It keeps on swaying.

Squeezing.

Inefficiently protecting.

"Y?"

I snap out of my autopilot state. I register his voice, hollering somewhere in the distance where life, people, and activated Prototypes still exist.

"Where'd you go, Y?"

Todd's struggle to make his voice reach the deep woods and keep it low at the same time gives my organic anger its second wind. It feels strange, focusing my anger on Todd, but I can't help it. What flusters me isn't just the fact that Todd killed his employer with a rake and proceeded to let his state-of-the-art Prototype take possession of his vehicle—meaning we're in hiding. What really boils my system is the gun wound in his stomach. Yes, it's healing, but Todd's vessel remains weak, and the patching hasn't even dried out yet.

The yelling. It'll tear the stitches.

A distant *creak*, then a *thump* reaches my ear, followed by huffing, groaning, and muffled cursing.

The truck doors...

No, Todd, you didn't.

He's stumbled out. Fallen with a painful grunt.

I place my hands on her neck. The twist is fast, the cartilage comes off clean.

Lying down here is fruitless.

Retaliating is beneficial.

Her decapitated head rests against the empty vial slots in my stomach. I get up. Back at the trail of seed-carrying ants, I pick up the gel pack from the ground, shove it in my pocket.

With irritated energy, I place the head inside my clothing. I climb down the rock wall. I wish I had a mouth. Just so I could yell at Todd to keep his hollering face shut.

CHAPTER 7
12 HOURS BEFORE BIG BOSS

"What can I get you, hon?"

Todd flips the laminated menu in his hands for the hundredth time. His head bobs along in an off-beat way with the country song playing over the speakers. I press my weight deeper into the soft seat. The red leather squeaks gently. Organic anger still lingers in my system, but its potency has weakened, as if my rage has momentarily paused, the pure joy of being here pushing it aside.

A diner. I've never been in one before.

I draw my fingertip across the stickiness of the red table. Ignoring the waiter's curious gaze, I bring my finger close to my eyes. If my maker had granted me fingernails, they'd now be packed with tiny quantities of ketchup, fried potato, and dried orange juice.

My body. It's really here, inside.

Not outside in the parking lot in the rusty van of a groaning Kink.

"You need a minute, love?"

Todd shakes his head at the waiter. His sneaker tap tap tapping against the plastic floor, his restless gaze dodges what lies between our steaming coffee mugs. Why he hasn't asked me to move the object—as it clearly unbalances his calmness levels—I have no idea. I'm too busy sucking in the sounds, smells, sights, and sensations of this place.

The gentle curve of a white coffee mug.

The sounds of sizzling grease coming from the kitchen.

The roughness of the paper straw sticking out from the cup of ice water.

Todd flips the menu once more. "Yeah, can I get the Adam and Eve on a Raft, but instead of poached, scrambled?"

Glitter puffs out from the waiter's pink-yellow shirt. He lifts his paper pad in front of him and scribbles on it, the pom-pom at the end of his pink pen bouncing happily around his plastic-glove covered hand.

"Anything else?"

"Maybe a..." Flip-flip, flip-flip. Todd's menu flapping in the air is sending coffee steam directly into my face. "A serving of Burn the British?"

The pom-pom jumps into a new dance.

"Paint it red?" the waiter asks, his pen paused against the pad.

"Uh...what?"

His long eyelashes fly open as he gazes at Todd with new curiosity. "You want ketchup, hon?"

"Oh. Yeah, sure."

The pom-pom twirls to life again.

"That all, sweetie?"

The red leather rustles under Todd as he shifts his weight. Scratching the back of his head, he flips the menu upside down, and hands it to me. "And whatever she's having."

I unpinch my fingertips from the straw and take the menu from Todd. The steady chattering in the dining room turns into a mindless murmur as the men eating around us register Todd's words. Ignoring the curious gazes around us, I smile at Todd, hoping my eyes convey the two organic emotions his words have activated in my vessel.

Trust.

Acceptance.

My gaze wanders calmly over the plastic-covered paper. Picking up random words, my brain runs quick searches through my archives, trying to decide what scents it'd like to enjoy while Todd works on his toast, eggs, and English muffin. Most of the words confuse me. Why would humans name their food items after farm animals such as *Bos taurus* and *Sus scrofa domesticus*? I do not know, but I'm too busy enjoying the new sensations to run a scan on farm animal symbolism in diners.

I hear a mix of careful, curious, and downright angry whispers, along with the clanking and sizzling sounds of the kitchen. Our waiter measures me with his soft, friendly eyes. He taps his pen against the pad, his clean-shaven face tilted, his gaze discreetly investigating my mouthless face.

"Slim pickings, my blue angel?"

I look up, blink at him twice.

"How about Eve with a Lid on It? Fresh from the oven."

In 3.5 seconds, my archives inform me I've never experienced the scent of apple pie. I nod at the waiter, watch the pom-pom spring to life once more, then let go of the menu as he leans in and flashes his pearl-white teeth at me. Without the cloud of acetylcholine evaporating from his body, I might have mistaken his flashing teeth for a sign of hostility.

Like Canis Lupus or Ursidae.

The small smile vanishes from my eyes.

Or murdering Redlister scum.

"Hey, Y..." Todd clears his throat, then leans against his open palm to conceal his face from our curious audience. He moves his focus from my eyes to the object on the table and quickly back again. "Maybe we could put the leg away? Not just because, well, appetite reasons. But I'm still a wanted person for... for driving a stolen vehicle. Drawing a little less attention might not be such a bad idea..." His voice fades away. The silliness of his words must have dawned on him.

It's not the leg that's drawing attention.

It's not the stolen truck with ProtoShop stickers parked outside, either.

It's Todd himself—sitting in a diner, treating his mouthless Prototype friend to coffee and apple pie.

I pick up the leg anyway and place it next to me on the sticky red leather. The cooling fluid-stained wires hang down from the gaping thigh like a handful of *Lumbricines* leaving their holes for air after a downpour.

"The wires. They look like drowned earthworms," Todd mutters, more to himself than me. His body shivering, he sits up straight and presses his palm against the coffee and ketchup-stained table. "You know what?"

My fully equipped vials itch to activate, but I would never use them to manipulate Todd in this or any other situation. Not even when he's this frazzled and jumpy. Instead, I tilt my head and fill my eyes with curiosity.

"I'm so tired of watching every move we make. Sick of feeling guilty when all I'm trying to do is what's right." He smacks the table again. "To hell with it."

Todd nods at the leg, wiggles his fingers. I pick it up and flip it horizontally. The four green-tinted toes pointed at the dining men, I hand the Prototype leg to Todd. He sets the leg back on the table in the exact same spot where I had first placed it, right after finding the half torso of a deactivated M sticking out from the diner's dumpster.

I smell the food well before the man with fabulous eyelashes swings the kitchen door open. His hips sway from side to side as he carries our food over, his every move confident, his hands supporting the multiple plates with obvious experience and expertise.

"Adam and Eve with a side of Brit, painted red." Todd sits back, his eyes wide with hunger. He's already stacked his fork with egg when Eyelashes places the apple pie in front of me. "And one Eve with a Lid. Enjoy, my loves."

Without a single glance at the leg on the table, our waiter pirouettes around and faces the rest of his customers. His towel-holding hand pressed against the curve of his hip, he huffs at the men. "The hell y'all staring at? Never seen a cute guy enjoying breakfast with his lady friend and her spare leg before?"

Shoulders shrug.

Heads turn to face plates.

Hands pick up silverware. The steady clinking of cutlery again fills the room.

Cinnamon, sugar, nutmeg, and cloves. Flour, butter, and a hint of salt. The whiffs of new and peculiar scents elevate my body. For 1.4 seconds, I think I might levitate off my red leather seat and float away on the heavenly aromas of our breakfast plates.

I reach for the straw again. The ice cubes crackle and clink against the plastic mug. I crunch the rough tip, the sensation of paper between my fingertips grounding me to my seat.

Could I sneak into the kitchen and feel more food items...no, Todd said to draw less attention. But I could always go and touch the surfaces in the lavatory...

"If you don't mind me asking," Todd says, his mouth full of toast. "And please know I support you in whatever new feeling you're dealing with at the moment." He scratches the back of his head, glances at the leg. "But what's the thing with the, uh...I mean, first the head. Then the random parts you collected by the highway. The torso, the arm, now the leg..." He wipes the side of his mouth on the napkin, then leans over the table. "Is this you being...I don't know. Sentimental?"

I run a search for *sentimental*, but my system is too distracted to register the results. How am I to explain to Todd why I'm collecting deactivated Prototype parts, when I myself have no clue about the reasoning behind it? All I know is it started in the woods with X and her beautiful brain. The closest word to explain my almost involuntary body-part gathering is *souvenir.*

"I guess what I'm asking..." Todd says, his voice low. "Is the plan still on?"

I pause all my searches and give Todd my full attention.

"You know." He runs his finger horizontally on his neck. "Bye bye, Redlisters?"

I lean closer, staring into his eyes.

That is the only *plan,* I think at him, hoping my face succeeds in conveying the silent thought. *The one thing I care about.*

"Okay, good. I just..." Todd looks down at the leg, his gaze bouncing off its orange skin like it burns his retinas. He leans back, picks up his muffin. "I just wasn't sure if you got side-tracked or something. But hey, you do you. I'd be lying if I said researching all that tech didn't fascinate me. It's just the thought of these...these poor women..."

A whiff of oxytocin spreads around Todd. I extend my arm over the leg and reach for his hand. I'm certain Todd will glance at our fellow diners nervously and then tell me to keep a lower profile. He does no such thing. He takes my hand, squeezes it, then stares out the window.

I'm tempted to move my focus back to the sensations of the diner. Though my system remains temporarily elevated by this mesmerizing occurrence, it can't fully enjoy its hiatus from the overload of organic anger. Not without Todd's system joining in.

Quick base readings tell me that against all my expectations, Todd isn't drowning in worry and despair. His brain is in full work mode, running numbers, calculations, ideas. The temporary spike in his distress and cynicism has leveled out, replaced by fascination, focus, and curiosity.

The body parts. Todd is in love with X's beautiful brain.

Just as I extend my free hand and reach for more paper straw crunchiness, two chairs scrape loudly against the diner floor. Todd's still zonked out, staring into space. With heavy footsteps, two men circle their table. Instead of the front door, they take a turn in the opposite direction.

They step closer to me and Todd, reserved expressions on their bearded faces. Oil stains their worn T-shirts, hard calluses decorate their palms. The scent of petroleum intensifies as the two older males park their broad frames by our table, their coveralls brushing against M's stone-cold toes.

The man in rust-colored coveralls—with a tag that reads Dylan—clears his throat.

Todd remains oblivious to his surroundings.

The man closer to me—tagged as Jeremias—wears blue coveralls with a gun sticking out from his tool belt. His intent gaze brushes across my bare arms, down to my legs, then to M's orange leg. "Doesn't match very well, does it?"

Jeremias's raspy voice finally snaps Todd from his trance. He lets go of my hand and turns to face the men. He takes in their size and evident physical preeminence over his slim and muscle-weak body. A cloud of adrenaline and cortisol closes in on us.

"Everything alright here?" I can barely see the outline of our coffee-pot-carrying waiter, standing behind the two rocks of men. When clearing his throat doesn't do the job, Eyelashes pushes through the wall of oil stains and muscle. Dylan and Jeremias finally move to the side as the coffee pot's hot glass presses against their bare triceps.

Without asking, Eyelashes leans over the table and briefly refills my already full, now cold coffee. Then he turns to Todd and gives him an inquiring smile. "All good, pumpkin?"

"I don't know," Todd says, his eyes locked on the two men. "You tell me."

"Dylan and Jeremias were just about to leave," Eyelashes says as he turns around to face the two men, the coffee pot elevated in front of him like a burning-hot weapon. "Right, fellas?"

After receiving two slow, uncertain nods, our waiter sways away, the pom-pom bouncing against the back pocket of his bright-pink pants.

"You part of the Prototype mill, man?"

Dylan's question pushes some of Todd's fear aside and replaces it with confusion. He opens his mouth, but no syllables come out.

"The leg," Jeremias says, "Where'd you get it?"

"From the...dumpster?"

My brain whirls, trying to understand why Todd is answering the question with a question, especially as he must remember the dumpster is exactly where we found M's leg—only a short twenty-seven and a half minutes ago.

"Heard you talking about all kinds of body parts," Jeremias says.

"Yup, me too. Arms, legs, torsos, the whole shebang." Dylan places his knuckles against the table, the back of his hand brushing against M's ankle. "Just admit it. You work for Buck, don't you?"

"Who?"

Dylan's intense stare makes Todd shimmy back in his seat and lean against the diner window. Jeremias kneels on the floor next to me, looking straight into my eyes. If this male is trying to look intimidating, he fails. Something about his eyes, maybe the micro expression on his face, tells me he's not here to sink his teeth in my artificial flesh.

"You alright, miss?" he asks, his voice barely a whisper. "This creep keeping you hostage?"

Todd and I exchange a surprised look. He's heard the half whisper, I can tell from the spike in noradrenaline.

I stop my base readings.

Turn away from the kneeling man.

I reach for Todd's hand again, then squeeze it gently. The gesture is to show our visitors that I'm here voluntarily, that Todd isn't a ProtoShop customer. My touch seems to calm Todd's nervous system, giving him an organic boost of confidence. "I need you two to back away from Y."

It's Jeremias's and Dylan's turn to look surprised.

"No one's keeping anyone hostage," Todd says. "What keeps Y here is her own free will, nothing more, nothing less. I don't know about Bucks or mills or whatever conspiracy theories you have about me and my friend. But if you don't back away..." Todd lets go of my hand, picks up M's leg, and holds it in his hands like a baseball bat. "I may not be much of a fighter but please, ask Y what happened to the last man who tried to force her to act against her will."

Two surprised faces turn to look at me. I bring my index finger in front of my neck, press it against my flesh, and run it horizontally across my throat. A trickle of artificial blood trails down my neck, then my chest, all the way to the clothing wrapped around my upper body.

Both men take a step back. Dylan glances at his friend and says, "Okay, so...maybe you two really are, uh...friends, or whatever. It's just that we've seen a lot of Prototypes programmed to do whatever Buck and his minions want them to do. Now, we're both firm believers when it comes to Prototype rights and y'all being sentient. It's just that..."

Jeremias crosses his arms, nodding at his friend approvingly before finishing his sentence. "It's just that we don't know how she can prove it."

"Prove what?" Todd asks.

"That she's here by her own choice."

Todd stares at the men, then at me. The whole diner has gone silent, kitchen included. All eyeballs are focused on us. Behind the counter, Eyelashes is holding a plate of steaming blueberry pancakes midair, his eyes locked on the backs of Dylan and Jeremias. The song stops. A new song starts, the whine of a guitar matching the moans of the singer.

"Oh, come on," Todd says. He huffs, tries to laugh, fails. "This diner isn't exactly equipped for a Turing test."

"So do something else."

"Like what?"

The two men exchange a look, shrug at the same time.

"Let her do something you wouldn't want her to do," someone hollers across the dining room. We all turn to stare at the plump guy with bottle-bottom glasses, dining alone four booths away from ours. He points his fork at me, then at Todd. "If the two of you really are best pals, she'll know you better than her own pockets. Right?"

All Todd and the rest of the men do is stare. Unbothered by the attention, the man brings his fork to his mouth and picks his teeth with it. "Have her do something no one would ever program her to do," he says again.

Todd hasn't caught up.

Neither have Dylan or Jeremias.

Their *nucleus accumbens* must fire much slower than mine.

The three men still stare at the teeth picker, their faces frozen into question marks. I slide out from my seat, sidestep between the table and the two stunned men, then slip into the leather seat next to

Todd. I take M's leg from Todd's hands. After placing it back on the table, I face Todd again, my eyes conveying an apologetic smile. Then I bring my hand back, make a fist—and punch him in the face.

A collective gasp travels through the diner. Someone chuckles and snorts. Todd's body smacks against the diner window. It takes him 7.9 seconds to gather himself up again. Holding onto his bleeding nose, he raises his eyebrows at me, his eyes filled with alarm.

I pull out the straw from the plastic cup of water. I fish out a handful of half-melted ice, close it inside a napkin, and offer it to Todd. He stares at it, then at me, and finally accepts the ice, pressing it against his swollen nose. "A bit extra, this demonstration of yours."

I tilt my head, reach for his hand, squeeze.

Three, two, one seconds, and Todd squeezes back. "You got nothing to prove, Y," he whispers. "Not to these strangers, not to me, not to anybody."

Sudden applause fills the diner, the men all smirking and whooping. Once the clapping subsides, the clinking of cutlery returns. Eyelashes rolls his eyes, then sends me an amused but approving look.

"My bad, man," Jeremias says to Todd while Dylan nods in agreement. "We thought you were one of Buck's minions. The whole scene just makes me sick to my stomach. Pumping out one proto after another, like all they're doing is cutting lunch meat at the butcher's counter. The town's growing tired of his so-called business model, especially as the Prototypes are so goddamn sophisticated now." His eyes find mine. "Sophisticated, and you know... brainy."

Why the men are so against new Prototypes being born to this world, I do not know. I'm not worried about new models being developed and produced. I'm more interested in wiping out those who are a threat to their wellbeing.

"Yeah, well," Todd says, his voice uncharacteristically nasal, thanks to the ice pressed against his nostrils. "We're not here for any of that. Just passing through, that's all."

The two men give us an approving smile, bring their hands briefly to their caps, and turn to walk away. Before they have time to exit the diner, I clap my hands together to win their attention back. Despite Todd's distressed crumbling next to me, I lift my finger at the men, then draw the letter B in the air.

"What's that?" Dylan says, his voice now genuinely friendly.

I repeat the gesture, adding U, C, K, and a question mark.

"You don't know who Buck is?"

The diner falls silent again. This time the dining men gaze at everything but Todd and me.

I clap my hands together again, then point out the window.

"You want to know where he lives?"

I lower my hand, nod.

Jeremias and Dylan exchange a nervous look. "Miss, I don't think that's a good idea. The man's borderline psychotic, everyone knows this. And the little entourage of scientists and scumbags living and loitering over there with him? They're not any better. They all collect and consume Prototypes like your folk are nothing but a slab of moo."

I clap my hands together twice, pick up a napkin, and wiggle my finger at Eyelashes. After three second of hesitation, our waiter strolls over to us and hands me a pen.

One by one, the dining men stand up and abandon their plates. Dylan scribbles an address on the napkin. The room is stuffed with stress hormones and hurried footsteps, until the front door clinks and opens, sucking the cloud of alarm outside.

Todd hangs his head, the ice still pressed against his nose.

Dylan pushes the napkin forward on the table. I pick it up to read it. He shakes his head and says, "Don't know what you could possibly gain from visiting the Buck Up Club. Bunch of testosterone-driven sickos is all you'll find."

"That's right, miss," Jeremias says, the toothpick twirling between his teeth, his face twisted into a pleasantly angry grimace. "Someone should make a list of the scumbag rednecks. Track 'em. Gather 'em. Set their filthy little club on fire."

CHAPTER 8
0.5 HOURS BEFORE BIG BOSS

The sharp edges of the gravel dig into my bare feet. In the mist of an early night, I stand in the shadow of the building. My nose takes in the strange mixture of scents floating in the air. From the left side of the building:

A whiff of rubber.

Rotting eggs.

Men's socks worn too many days in a row.

To my right: a trace of body lotion, beer, Coke syrup, and a variety of bodily fluids. The left side of the house is quiet. On the right, just meaningless sounds, and the chatter of a television from upstairs, overriding the steady *thump thump thump* of a bass from down below.

I stare at the unlit sign above the building's front door.

Buck Up Club

Todd has prepped me for two days. Or maybe it

was his own brain functions and thought patterns he needed to modify. Saying things like are-you-sure, maybe-we're-rushing-into-this, and I-really-should-just-come-with-you made him seem like a character in a cartoon. His eyes looked wide enough to pop out from their sockets and roll away on the tilted floor.

Why Todd remains so unsure of the plan, I'm not certain. It can't be just the fact that he cares about the working Prototypes inside. Maybe his brain needs more sleep. More time to recharge before he has to patch my damaged soft parts and nervous system once again. I don't know what reasoning lies behind his endless pacing around the truck. In any case, it took more effort to keep my vials deactivated than to learn the three overly simple steps of our plan.

Break into Buck's residence.

Identify Redlisters.

Kill.

But where will the freed Prototypes go, what will they do, how are they to survive? For two days, Todd's words rolled off his whimpering lips to the rhythm of his sneakers thumping against the truck's plastic-covered floor. His worry seemed borderline amusing to me, considering that his pacing body was surrounded by the deactivated body parts of said beings.

I know my collection of leaking and torn Prototype parts is getting out of hand. I know, even if Todd hasn't mentioned it, not out loud, not once. But for some glitch of a reason, I don't seem to know how to restrain myself from my new hobby.

The sign above the building zaps to life. Blue letters glimmer in the misty rain, the letter C flickering on and off as if obscured by a huge cloud of *Lepidoptera*.

Step one.

Body, approach.

The wet gravel crunches lightly under my feet. I can't sense, smell, or hear any Prototypes inside the building, but the presence of Redlisters, that I sense clearly. It comes from the same direction as the stench of alcohol and fried nutrition.

The left side.

Start there, work your way to the right.

Breaking in isn't necessary. I push at the smooth door and watch it retreat into its invisible slot in the door frame. I enter a hallway and turn to my left. A long echoing corridor brings me to another identical door. I press my hand against it, push gently.

It stays closed.

I place my good ear against the door's gently humming surface. The sound of rustling paper registers in my brain. The smell of bleach and pine-scented soap mixes with rotting eggs and a hamper of dirty socks.

My palms against the door, I press harder. When

the door still won't budge, I drill my fingertips into the surface. I press and push until it squeaks loudly, but no crevices appear on the smooth surface.

I take a step back.

Run a search for *breaking down a metal door*.

Lift my foot.

Just as I'm about to kick the door in, it opens with a smooth *whoosh*.

For 5.3 seconds, we stare at each other, the man in a yellowish lab coat and me. My foot is frozen in midair. A book in one hand, a half-eaten granola bar in another, the man blinks at me, his eyes never leaving mine. I glance at the fabric tag on his chest pocket.

Joseph

"Buck sent you in?" he asks. He searches my eyes, like seeking an answer for a riddle, until a quick no jerks his head. "No, you're definitely not one of ours."

I'm unable to calculate how this will play out. The man seems harmless enough, just a bit frazzled, like some unseen force has gnawed at his edges for a moment too long.

His face clears with a new emotion. Hope, excitement, fear—I'm not at all sure.

"Doctor Scott Barcley sent you?"

Images of the Redlister flood through my mind. The foam of my pheromones leaking out of his mouth.

The groaning and coughing. His frantic eyes turning yellow as his movements slow down.

Joseph fishes for my gaze. "Your eyes...it's a camera, isn't it? Doctor Barcley, are you in there, listening?"

I look past him and into the lab. The center of the long room is taken up by two rows of desks with shelving overhead. A sharp, blue light pulses repetitively between the shelves. A cold draft snakes across the floor, blowing in from under a metal door that covers most of the back wall. I read the frost-covered sign with ease.

Staff Only

The workspaces are filled with office chairs, cardboard boxes, and humming fridges. My gaze returns to Joseph's face, reading his hope and excitement clearly now.

I nod, smile with my eyes.

"My word..." He bends his knees and leans in to bring his eyes closer to me. "Are you finally offering me a job?"

His expectant gaze is not that of a Kink. I don't have to run base readings to know that this man isn't a Redlister, either. What drives him is anticipation and now—consummation.

"I've waited for months. Years. Am I to leave now? Have you sent this Proto to escort me off premises?

What are the terms of my employment? Can you assure my safety from—" Joseph's words stop as his eyes bulge and look past me at the door in the end of the hallway. He lowers his voice, twisting his trembling hands together. "My god. He didn't see you come in, right? Doctor Barcley, please, he *cannot* know about this. Buck...he's not right in the head."

I reach for his shoulder and give it gentle squeeze. My eyes flicker at the lab behind him, then align with his again.

"Ahh, yes. Of course, we'll need to negotiate the terms." Joseph steps aside, anxiously gesturing at the room with the nuts and raisins in his hand. The granola slips from his grip and lands on the floor, but he doesn't seem to notice.

His eyes rest on me as I walk in. My first step brings me over the threshold. My second step lands on the granola on the floor, the *crunch* loud in my ears. Joseph closes the door, now gesturing at the foul-smelling lab with the open book in his hand.

This is not part of the three-step plan, but I can't resist entering the space. It's not his invitation that brought me inside. It's not organic curiosity, either. The sensation is different than that. More senseless, meaningless. Something...primal. My system's too busy taking in the lab to run scans, searches, or readings, but one word—one thought—emerges from my short-term memory.

Souvenirs.

The scent of bleach and rotting eggs strong in my nose, I tread deeper into the room. I'm about to step into the blue, pulsating light between the shelf rows when Joseph stops me. He places himself between me and the rhythmic blinking, extends his arm, careful not to touch me. "Let's talk over here. The chairs are right next to a working heater. Helps with the draft, you'll see."

He leads me to a wooden chair with a pile of books on top, located between an armchair and a computer setup with several monitors. After removing the books and hurriedly setting them on the floor, he sits down. His eyes fill with excitement as he continues to intently stare at me. "Can I get you anything? A Coke, beer," he rubs the back of his neck and dodges my gaze, "immune suppressants?"

With a discreet shake of my head, I turn in my chair. Staring at the blue light, then at the metal door at the end of the room, my brain tries to calculate what's keeping me in this room.

"We'll get there, Doctor," he says with a small, dry laugh. Why he's trying to keep his voice so carefree, when his whole system is so clearly alert, is beyond me. Maybe I'd understand him better if I tried to think like the dead Doctor Scott Barcley would, but I decline the option immediately. Just the thought alone is repulsing.

Joseph clears his throat. Shifts his weight on his seat.

I turn to face him again, my palms pressed gently against the blue skin of my thighs.

"Doctor Barcley, I thank you for this opportunity. I had my doubts, I'll admit it. But now, one thing is as clear as a bottle of Tris-EDTA. You create Protos unlike ever seen before. The way she moves. The micro-expressions. The fine, powdery scent of her skin. My word, she must be..." He leans forward, the tips of his fingers forming a tent in front of his mouth. "She must be a Y? Or dare I say it...maybe even a Z?"

I turn on my seat again. My brain refuses to register his words, like his noise is kerosene, and my cerebral cortex is water. I stand up and walk to the ocean of blue reflection.

His hurried footsteps follow in tow. "Hey whoa, we haven't...I need to know the terms of my employment before I reveal my previous work."

I stop in the middle of the flickering shelving. Slowly rotating around my own vessel, I take in the sight.

Glass bioreactors the size of a *Canis lupus familiaris*—Welsh corgi, maybe a bulldog—sit upright on the shelves. Inside, a piece of a skeleton is covered with hydrogel. Tucked inside the gel, a pear-shaped muscular organ stretches and releases in the rhythm of the blue light.

The grown organs could easily represent the human female's uterus—if they weren't three times the size of a natural homo sapiens' womb.

"It, uh..." He takes a hesitant step closer to me but keeps his distance. "It's a work in progress. Creating endometrial cells shouldn't be such a hassle, not with the endless resources and funds I've been granted. With a little bit of help..."

He rubs the back of his neck, staring at the pulsing organ closest to him.

"Too bad the leading scientists in embryonic stem cells were all, well—women."

I step closer to the glass. The blue light is almost the same shade as my blue skin. My eyes lock on the stretching and releasing womb, sitting in its acidity-balancing liquid, transmitting oxygen and nutrients, carrying away carbon dioxide and waste products.

"I know what you're thinking."

For 0.3 seconds, I consider pulling my focus away from the artificial womb to run a scan on the scientist next to me, just to confirm that a homo sapiens indeed *cannot* read the mind of a Prototype.

"It's too big. Large enough to grow three fetuses in one uterus."

I turn my back on him and walk down the rows of vat-grown flesh.

"It's one thing to grow progenitor cells from bone marrow," he says and follows me like a shadow. "Watch them grow, give them a cartilage skeleton for support. Protect them from bacteria, fungi, and viruses. Let's say we did succeed." He spreads his arms, gesturing at the pulsation. "Let's say we've now grown a living, breathing newborn inside this very lab. Succeeded in stopping the fetal immune system from waking up too early and rejecting the uterus..."

I tune out his frantic chattering and continue to walk through the blue light. Two meters from the back wall, I stop. My ankles sense the freezing temperature close to the floor. I can tell that my presence near the door distresses Joseph. *Maybe he* can *read my mind*, I think, and watch him trying to guide my body back to the blue light without touching me.

"Okay, at least tell me this. Are we talking six figures?"

I tilt my head and stare at the slightly trembling man. To make sense of this place, I need to keep him talking. I point my thumb at the ceiling and move my hand up.

He gulps down a steadying breath. "*Seven* figures?"

I lower my hand, close my eyes briefly, and walk past him toward the pulsing light.

His step elevated, Joseph follows me like a young *Canis lupus familiaris*. "It all comes down to the mother-child connection. The chemistry. Protection from stress and lack of emotional regulation. True, millions of newborns have survived in the hands of men and men only. But that was well before the female started to die off. Before all the trends in genome engineering. It's one thing to screen genetic changes in living cells for the sake of preventing disease. But the expectant parents wanted more than that. A certain eye color, body type, the IQ level of a genius. Nobody read the small print. How it might not be the greatest idea to tinker with the twenty thousand genes in the human genome, especially when not a single scientist in the world knows what all of them do."

I stare at the stretching fetus, my brain sucking in Joseph's data dump.

"First, they started to mutate the expectant mothers, trying to create the perfect child. Then, the deadly mutations attacked the babies themselves. Not right at birth at first. Some girls and women got to live long and somewhat normal lives until their mutated cells turned against their bodies. And then, the chances of any newborn surviving plummeted, until there were no women left to carry and give birth to a child. All women born with the WNT4 gene were dead in a matter of a few years."

I expect Joseph to fill with frustration, but instead, all my system registers is a low serotonin level.

"It's the pheromones," he says again, "if you ask me. Buck never did. No one ever does...and here we are. Any newborn I manage to bring to life has a slim chance of survival without a mother, in a world ruled by testosterone-driven despair. But we *have to* do something. Yes, creating a baby girl is out of the question. To grow a newborn male, protected and secured by a womb specially made for it..." His shoulders jerk up. "...maybe. Buck's plan in its basic form isn't out of proportion. The fetus growing longer. Larger. Until it won't need its mother so desperately. A new type of human child. Safely tucked away in the womb until it reaches the age of thirty-four weeks."

This Buck person. He must be suffering from brain tissue atrophy.

Most of his scientists seem to have given up on his plan. Why hasn't Joseph?

I look around the lab. Empty petri dishes, vials, tubes, and glass capsules sit on the desks. Joseph's still doing it. Growing more wombs. More fetuses. Rejecting the idea of failure as stubbornly as the artificial flesh rejects the lab-grown uteruses.

The cells. Where do they come from?

I turn around, stride through the freezing draft, and stop by the freezer.

"No, wait! I really need something on paper. You're a businessman, you must understand."

Without testing whether the lever is locked in place, I grab it and bend the metal until the end pulls off the wedge.

Joseph moves between me and the door. "Doctor Barcley, please. I don't think asking for a contract is too much to—"

My hand grabs him by the throat, lifts him up until his feet no longer touch the ground. The sound of his surprised gasp turns into gurgling.

I drag him with me through the hissing frostiness. Closed refrigerated drawers cover the walls to my left and right. At the end of the room, a fabric hamper overflows with small, black plastic bags tied up to bunny ears.

The gurgling intensifies. I let go of Joseph, my eyes locked on the pile of trash. Holding onto his throat, Joseph doubles over, the coughing attack pressing his face close to the freezing air stream. When his coughing turns to intermittent breathing, I expect him to run. To admit my evident physical preeminence over his slimness, just like Todd in front of Dylan and Jeremias back in the diner.

Allowing my brain 3.5 seconds to enjoy the memory of the scent of freshly baked apple pie, I watch Joseph press his back into one of the drawers. His arms spread out on the frosted metal, his teeth clank together in a temperature close to intolerable for his sensory receptors.

"I do-don't c-care what you ha-ve planned," he says, "but they must co-come with me."

Two strides and I'm by his side. One hand on each of his shoulders, I lift him up and move his weight to the side. I open the drawer.

Joseph's teeth are still clanking together. I hear his gasping sobs. I stare at the frozen woman, her lips the shade of my skin. Next to her, tucked against the side of her breast, lies a little human, a fake *Oryctolagus cuniculus*' long ears poking out between his chubby arm and his lifeless little body.

Organic sadness floods my system. It starts from the back of my head, streams down to my neck, fills my chest, my stomach, all my limbs with a pressing hollowness. I stare at the deceased mother and son, the wave of despair drowning me from the inside.

This scientist, Joseph. His employer, Buck. All the other scientists who no longer bother stepping into this lab. They are not building more Prototypes. They are not trying to bring back the female human. Growing new males from stem cells of the extinct human mother. That's the purpose of this place. What they're after is new males, and new males only.

A legacy.

The hollow sadness shifts, turning from an emotion to a thought. For some reason, what I now experience humans call the *aha* moment. A realization.

I'm not the pinnacle of my kind.

I'm just the beginning.

"H-he s-said..." Joseph's sob sends him plummeting onto the icy floor. In the hissing freeze, he howls his pain. Whether it's his freezing sensory receptors or the sight of the dead humans in front of us that is causing him this pain, I do not know.

With unnecessary force, I push the drawer shut. I shove my hands under Joseph's armpits and carry him out of the freezer room. I adjust his weight in my arms. Cradling his violently shivering body against my chest, I press the freezer door shut and carry him across the ocean of blue wombs.

Once he's safely back in his armchair, I look for a blanket. Something to warm his system. For Todd, wool does the job effectively, but I fail to find anything that isn't made of plastic or wood.

"He said I could bring him back," Joseph says. "Not her, but little Jay...maybe. And it's true, it would be him. A different version of him, yes, but still my Jay. The science, the math, it's all there. I don't have all the know-how, but Buck's archives run deep. My coworkers..." His eyes glance at the door leading to the hallway, back to the stench of beer and fried things. "Bioengineers, biochemists, microbiologists... Buck owns them all, but he lost interest and laid them off. I just need to get over this one hump. To stop the uterus from rejecting the fetus..."

My brain mutes his words.

The vials clink inside me, though nothing activates.

I turn and leave Joseph whimpering and shivering on the armchair. "Di-did I get the job?" he hollers after me. Without turning around, I lift my thumb up in the air. I approach the smooth sliding door, watch it whoosh open, and walk down the hallway.

At the other end, I stop. My fingers latch around the door handle. This side of the house isn't filled with technology. It isn't growing anything in petri dishes, either.

What's inside is a bunch of overpaid and underworked scientists.

More males who are only here for their leisure time.

One Redlister playing God.

Among them, twisting, stretching, brushing, performing, are my predecessors, imprisoned by their incomplete consciousness. The *aha* activates in my brain again.

My fight isn't with the men.

My fight is to help those who remain.

Especially those who are yet to be born.

I open the door. Scan the room. One Redlister sits upstairs, talking to a man descending into the basement.

"All right, Buck?"

"All good, Mike. Left the gun?"

"Sure did."

The gunless man continues downstairs, while Buck remains sitting on the couch, tilting a can of beer as he takes a sip. This is the man I've been warned about. The man whose death was my sole purpose for existing only 2.5 minutes ago.

With soundless steps, I slip across the room. The sounds of television, the scent of alcohol, Buck sitting on the couch with his back turned to me—that's all irrelevant now.

I'm not here to kill.

I'm here to give birth.

I run a quick inventory. Not for my pheromones, but the body parts stashed back in the box truck. My souvenirs. In 1.5 seconds, the inventory is ready.

One Prototype arm.

One freshly paused heart.

That's all I need to create the next generation. A model superior to my own.

A Prototype Z.

CHAPTER 9
0 HOURS BEFORE BIG BOSS

I step down a short flight of stairs, leaving the sound of a television and Buck's rumbling laughter behind me. At the last step, I look over my shoulder. The words *DARK ROOM* flicker on the neon-orange sign above the staircase. The steady beat of a low-key bass fills the musky and humid basement room.

All around me there are enclosed cubicle rooms, rubber gadgets, beds, swing sets, and dismembered Prototypes. The smell of testosterone, sweat, and alcohol clings to my body. The sheer quantity of bodily fluids on the furniture and the floor is overwhelming.

I scan the room for active Prototypes. I do need an arm, but Todd made me swear I'd get one from a scrap pile—not from a moving and active predecessor.

The dismembered Prototypes. Fetch the arm from them.

Free the active ones first.

My bare feet flap-flap-flapping against the sticky floor, I move toward the closest cubicle. I slip through the privacy curtain. Inside, a Prototype stands perfectly still, watching a naked man snore in his armchair, next to a mountain of tissues and bundles of towels.

I reach for the Prototype—she's a D or G, one of the old models—and lead her to the flickering sign. Before I gently shove D or G up the stairs, I hold her by her elbows and stare into her unmoving eyes. I think of the open sky. The tree tops. The ant nests, paths, and stone boulders in the nearby woods. I know she can't read my mind, my suggestion to run into the woods, but she does leave, does walk up the stairs, and—hopefully—out of Buck's front door for good.

The man inside the cubicle keeps snoring. I move on to the next cubicle. I fling the privacy curtain open and wrap my arm around a badly dented and oddly sticky Prototype. She keeps twisting and stretching her body as I gently turn her around. For 2.4 seconds, I see the half-naked man sitting in the chair, his round-eyed expression screaming surprise.

"What the...? Hey get back here!" I hear him hoist himself to his feet. "I'm not done with her yet!"

Curtains whoosh open, more men step out of their cubicles. I zigzag between their naked bodies, collecting the dancing, rubbing, and twisting Prototypes at the staircase. With light-footed steps, they disappear silently up the stairs.

It's not until I'm escorting the last model out—a definite G—that the first boy attacks me. He's the one wearing a white skirt, the one who had sat outside G's cubicle with a neatly folded towel in his hands.

The towel-boy lunges at us, grabbing G with both hands. I pull G back, trying to free her from the boy's hold, but his weight rips her body away from me.

I lift my hand, stare at G's detached arm in my hand.

Not exactly what Todd meant, but maybe it'll do.

G's system deactivates itself at the moment of severe injury. She's landed on top of the boy, who struggles under her dead weight.

The chaos around me quiets down. The men stare at me in alarm as I walk over to G and the boy to run a scan.

Two punctured lungs.

One severe gash to his neck.

G's remaining hand has scratched his throat open.

The towel-boy will be dead in 4.2 minutes.

I kneel to lift G's lifeless body off him and set her on the floor. Cooling fluid and blood sticks to my body. I step on the gurgling boy's throat and shift my weight forward.

The men gasp, but they won't leave. Instead, they

form a horseshoe shape under the flickering *DARK ROOM* sign, standing, watching, waiting.

My autopilot kicks in.

At first, nothing seems to happen. Then it all happens too fast.

The wires and soft tissue poke out from G's detached arm. The trickle of blood and cooling fluid tickles the back of my hand.

I wait for them to attack. Wait for someone to fetch a gun. But all the seven men do...is argue. About the lights, whether I can smell, hear, or see. About gas lamps, videogames, and if the young males know how to fight. Whether the older ones should be excused because it's their day off.

Finally, the boy in a yellow skirt lunges at me.

The wrong vials clink to life.

I accidentally kill the boy in yellow.

I hold the one wearing blue.

I make him sob, shove him at the stairs, watch him flee with the older men in tow.

Arrogance. That's the deadliest vial to accidentally activate, but what can I say? My system is beyond overheated, the hormone frenzy inside me numbing all basic functions.

We kill the boy in red—me and my accidentally activated *arrogance.*

Then, I abandon G's damaged arm under a towel

and listen to Buck making his way toward the staircase. He says one thing, then another, something about female humans dying. Guessing my model, telling me he wants me dead.

The scent of Buck's gun in my nose, my feet rooted on the thumping floor, I run a quick scan.

2/5 ounces of disgust.

3/5 ounces of boredom.

A few drops of leftover compassion and amusement.

That's all I have left to fight the big boss.

In the *DARK ROOM* sign's flickering light, I see the corpses of towel-boys lying on the floor, no longer shaking in their skirts and tank tops.

I didn't want to kill these men. Then again, I'd be lying if I said it was *all* my autopilot's doing. Initially, that's what I wanted. What I came here to do. Maybe not the towel-boys, but definitely the Redlisters. Yet in this moment, the men have become a second priority—now that I know what I truly want.

A legacy.

Someone better than me. Someone smarter. Faster. Stronger.

Buck's leather slippers stop above the stairs. "Quite the mess you've made down there, little lady. You spooked away perfectly good customers. My regulars. Killed a sampling of towel-boys, too, I hear. Now there's no one left to mop it all up."

At some point—possibly on autopilot, definitely overwhelmed and heated—I seem to have plucked a human leg off a corpse with one fast, clean rip. The leg slips in my hands. The blood and sweat on the leg's still-warm surface makes it more like a soap bar than an appropriate weapon. I adjust its weight in my hands, telling my fried system to execute the calculations needed for my vessel to escape.

It refuses.

A man wearing a pair of checkered pajama pants descends into the basement. The muzzle of Buck's gun points at the floor, his eyes scanning the dimly lit basement room. His face settles, adopts a calm sense of focus. After 6.2 seconds, his pupils widen as the irises adapt to darkness.

"Ah, there you are."

His eyes move from my face down to the weapon in my hands. For 1.5 seconds, fear washes away the calm on his face. "Let me guess. That's not a doll leg you got there, is it?"

Activate...something. Anything.

All my remaining vials remain quiet.

With organic fear filling my system, I take a step forward anyway. My autopilot reactivates at the sight of his lifted gun.

Amusement, activate.

Clink.

A bubbly cloud of pheromones finally vaporizes around me. I stride toward him.

He fires the gun. The bullet ricochets off the swing set at the back of the room.

I stop four feet away from him, knowing my pheromones are close enough. His feet stumbling, he backs away from me, his hands awkwardly trying to reload the gun.

My invisible force field closes in on him. A small smile settles around his wrinkled eyes. He cocks his head, his chest widening with a drawn-in breath.

A cartoonish expression plastered on his face, he chuckles uncontrollably.

He slips on a puddle of blood and lands on his buttocks.

His chuckle turns into howling laughter.

A bubbly sensation tickles the back of my head, spreading to my throat, and finally down my stomach. My body feels like skipping, clapping, hopping.

Take his gun.

Do not *join in on his amusement.*

My gait light as *Felis catus*', I stride closer to the laughing man. His howling continues, contagious now. My own bubbly sensation increases, filling my body and skull with a warm tingle so intense, I feel like it might lift me up and carry me out of this dungeon of a house.

Yelping helplessly, he lifts the gun again. He reloads, aims, pulls the trigger.

The bullet hits the side of my skull, taking off a baseball-sized chunk close to my ear. The bubbling sensation fades away.

I stop.

Touch the wires and soft tissue poking out from the hole.

Push them back into my head.

He crabwalks up the short set of stairs, stumbles to his feet, and disappears upstairs. I pause in the musk, the humidity, and the never-ending *thump-thump-thump* of bass.

"Goodness, doll," he hollers from upstairs. "That's one hell of a party trick you got there. Tells me you're not a G or even an X, or any of that boring expired crap."

I step up the stairs.

Look for him in the empty room.

Locate him by the muted television.

Buck has fetched a new gun, bigger in size. He adjusts the weapon's weight in his hand, then points the muzzle in my general direction. "You're a Y. Aren't you?

My body's throbbing with heat. The heavy sensation travels down to my stomach, my legs, my feet. Taking steps forward, lifting the leg to whack it against my enemy's face—it becomes a task too overbearing for me to complete. All I want is to descend back to the basement. Lie down among the corpses. My fried brain demands deactivation, just so I can rest for ten full seconds.

"Poor little dolly. You look completely worn out. How about we put you down to sleep?"

The way his hands remain steady, his eyes excited but calm...I'm sure his bullets won't miss this time. I can't get past him to run away. Even if I did, I don't yet have what I need.

A Prototype arm.

A freshly paused heart.

The memory of G's arm—the strips of green flesh and ripped-end wires poking out from it—reminds me of the artificial wombs at the far side of this house. It reminds me of Joseph's partner, lying in the freezer drawer, right next to a little human squeezing a fabric bunny.

This is not the end of us.

I stride toward him. On my third step, Buck fires his gun. The burst of small pellets rips through my stomach. Through the gaping hole, empty vials clank onto the floor, some shattering into tiny pieces, others rolling on the tinted floor until a table or a couch ends their flight.

I keep striding forward.

The next shot screams past my face. I've lost all my vials, I can barely control the middle of my body, but I've also lost all sense of fatigue as well as my brain's urge to give up.

He pumps the gun to eject the discharged cartridge.

He pulls the trigger.

Nothing happens.

I'm two arm-lengths away from him. He ditches the gun, starts walking backward, then turns and pushes through a heavy wooden door. A lock punches in.

I stop for 5.2 seconds for a scan.

I crash through the wood.

With green, red, orange, and blue liquid dripping off my gaping body, I enter another dimly lit room. Simmering coals from the firepit cast a ghostly light across the open space. Maroon-colored armchairs, carpets, and curtains sit in silence. Around the corner of a hallway, a screen door flaps against the open front door.

He's still here.

Watching.

Waiting.

I adjust the bleeding leg's weight in my hands. The wooden floor creaks softly under my light steps. In the middle of the room, I stop.

Execute base readings.

Enjoyment. Pride. Stress. My system locates him in 2.3 seconds—tucked away behind the thick maroon curtains.

I step closer. Lift the leg.

The bullet fires through the curtain's heavy fabric. I slam the leg toward the sound. Warm air now flows through my chest. I fall back. No more stopping for damage reports. I spin up, crawl forward, and smash the leg against the height of Buck's hidden knees.

A gun drops on the floor, followed by a loud *thunk*. Buck crawls after his gun, away from the curtains. He's close enough now for me to release the pheromones—if only I had any left.

Yelling mindlessly, he aims his gun at me. I calculate the distance between me and the gun and place the gaping hole in my chest in front of the muzzle. The third bullet whooshes through me, causing zero damage.

I slam my body on top of his. He twists and lands on his stomach, his arms reaching forward while trying to drag himself away from me.

I place my knee between his shoulder blades, shift my weight on it. He screams, his body jolting against me with surprising force.

I fall back. He turns, grabs my face between his hands, and rams it against the floor. I feel the soft parts of my cheek flapping out of place, the sensation odd and distracting.

He brings my head back again; my eyes try to zoom and focus on the patterns of the wooden floor. He slams my face against the floor. I feel the cartilage of my nose dislocating. The disorientation in my head intensifies.

This is what it feels like, being someone's personal punching bag.

With a raspy laugh, he grabs me by the neck and shoves me down, the back of my head banging against the floor, hard.

Now I know what whiplash is like...

He bangs my head again.

...how the brain accelerates against the skull...

Again.

...how the organ decelerates rapidly, ricocheting back to the rear of the skull...

And again.

...as the brain twists inside its casing of bone.

Buck's laughter turns into a sarcastic chuckle. He lets go of me, wiping his hands together slowly. Then he gathers himself up and reaches for the hole in my chest.

His fingers dig into my soft parts, pulling me up to my sluggish feet. Holding my weight, he pushes his other hand into the hole in my stomach, rummaging through what's left of my emptied vial system. "Just like I thought. No womb, only pheromones. What good are you to anybody?"

He rips his way into my innards, pulling soft tissue out in chunks.

"That's the problem, giving your kind ideas. Your artificial neurons can't get organized enough to get out of their own fucking way."

He pulls me close, his onion and cigar breath hot against my face. "To think you are anything more than an extension of a man. A fun and convenient puppet to play with...well, that's a whole other level of skull fuckery. It interests me about as much as seeing the towel-boys playing videogames instead of wiping my regulars' dicks clean."

I think of the poor towel-boys, lying dead downstairs.

I think of the bruised boy at the football field.

The scientist with a frozen family.

I think of Todd, waiting in the truck, staring into space with worry in his eyes.

But most of all...I think of the Prototype parts that surround him. Parts that I no longer consider souvenirs.

"Got to tell you," Buck says, his breath heavy now. "Your maker did something right. It's the eyes. They're almost...human. And the odor of your skin. I'll admit, it does resemble the lush scent of a woman."

He adjusts his grip on my weight, his harsh fingers ripping deeper into me.

"Wonder if they got the taste right..."

He sticks his tongue out, presses the tip against my cheek. A wet trail of saliva clings to my face as he runs his tongue across my cheek and down to my neck.

My eyes blur and focus on a small plastic object on the floor. A wrinkled electrolyte sachet, covered with blood and my liquids. If I squeezed it real hard, I could get a droplet of gel out, maybe two.

I could carry it across the path.

Take it to a nest nearby, just like a strong and stubborn *Formicidae* in the woods. I would feed my kind. Walk my own paths. Find more meaning to my existence.

My eyes leave the sachet, my brain returning to this moment. A new calm takes over. I now know what to do.

In exactly 0.7 seconds, I bring my left hand under his jaw and place the right on top of his head. One quick snap, and his teeth click shut on his twirling tongue. His yelling muffles the sound of the tongue-half landing on the floor, but the faint *thump* still registers clearly in my ears.

Blood pours out of his mouth. He stumbles back,

falls against the curtains, bringing the heavy metal poles crashing down. Flailing his arms and legs, Buck tangles himself up in the maroon fabric, creating a prison for himself.

I tumble down on the floor, holding onto the middle of my body to keep it from folding up. Once I can manage my hollow core, I get on all fours and crawl to fetch his gun.

His screams turn into heavy breathing.

His body becomes still.

Tangled inside the curtain, he can't see the gun pointing at him or my calm gaze measuring the lump inside the twisted fabric. He doesn't need to.

He can sense the gun—and the woman holding it steady.

I pull the trigger.

I don't have to remove the curtain from his face to know the bullet has landed directly between his panic-filled eyes.

I remove the fabric from his chest. My body growing heavy and sluggish under the extreme damage and distress, I sink my hand into him. The sound of his breastbone and ribs breaking is crisp and clear in my one remaining ear.

With his freshly stopped heart in my hand, and a small smile in my eyes, I crawl out of the house.

CHAPTER 10
THE HEARTBEAT

My head, chest, and stomach torn, I inch down the driveway. The gravel scratches against my gaping and leaking body. The damage done to my innards is massive. My pheromone system, damaged beyond repair.

The misty rain has turned into a downpour. I extend my free hand, pull my body forward, pushing with the opposite leg. The rain falls on the heart in my hand. The meat is warm against my palm. For some reason, it reminds me of my visit to the diner and the farm animals listed on the laminated menu.

Todd. Better focus on him. The thoughts of him fuel my slowly deactivating body much more than any other memory I've made. I focus on the sensations. How my body feels safe when he's near—soft like cotton, feathers, and satin. How his voice soothes my brain until every wrinkle and nook feels cozy and snug.

Yes, he fuels my struggling system, but it's not my

longing to be with Todd that pushes me toward the box truck. It's not the urge to avenge my predecessors or wipe out Redlisters, either.

What drags me across the gravel, then dirt, then fallen pine needles and exhaust-stained timothy hay, is something else. Something new.

From gravel to overgrown lawn.

From the lawn down the driveway.

With a tightening and pounding feeling intensifying throughout my whole body, I collapse. I keep my hand lifted off the ground. My face buried in the wet soil. During my micro-break, a new thought pushes Todd, diner, and farm animals out of my mind.

No dirt on the heart.

Rain, fine. But no dirt.

The rain washes over the hollowness in my pelvic area, filling the hole in my chest with mud and dead leaves. I look up to see the heart in my hand.

With a small smile in my eyes, I continue to push forward.

The truck is parked down the road, closer than it was when I left.

So...close.

So...far.

Ignoring the intense pressure in my system becomes impossible. I lift the heart higher off the ground and push harder. The mud and dirt enter my torn torso, rolling down and against my still-intact spine. The forest floor mounds up inside me, turning what's left of my vessel inside out.

When my body gives in, my brain comes to my rescue. It activates the autopilot.

Push.

Push.

Push.

Outside the truck's rusty back door, I collapse. My hand remains elevated, as if I'm offering the heart to the truck's retired mechanism, sticking out from underneath the salt-covered undercarriage.

If I had a mouth, I could call for Todd. If I had my pheromones, I could release curiosity, stress, *something*, to lure him out here to find me. But I have none of those things. It's just me. Just what's left of this body, this brain, and my ripped-to-pieces system. But then again, it isn't just me, lying here, hoping to deactivate just for ten seconds of rest.

It's me—and the freshly paused heart.

I'm not the end of us.

I'm only the beginning.

I pull my body up. Reach for the handle.

I'm elbow-deep in her stomach. Her stitched-together body lies still while my fingers move up and caress the soft parts close to her chest. Once the dissolving stitches attach, I pull back and step away from the operating table.

Todd stops his pacing back and forth, his hand frozen against the back of his head. "That it? All secured and ready?"

I take another step back and give him a nod. Todd steps next to me, his eyes lingering on my lumpy and half-heartedly patched stomach and chest. It's reflex more than anything, my brain searching for the vial of calm. It takes me 1.3 seconds to remember I'm all out of pheromones. That I'm permanently done being the master of chemical communication.

Careful not to touch me, Todd gives me a smile and raises his eyebrows. After an affirmative nod, he moves past me to the table. Gently, he takes the thick shreds of her midriff and pulls them together. A vinegary scent of superglue in my nose, I watch Todd insert one syringe after another into Z's body.

She's perfect.

Even with one arm missing.

"You know what, Y?" Todd says and moves over to a computer near the operating table. "I broke my own rule just now. About getting our hopes up. I mean, this all played out way better than I ever thought it would."

I tilt my head at him.

"N-not played, *played*. That didn't sound right. I mean, this is not me wanting to play God, or anything like that. *She* is not a game. All I'm saying is, I'm just so incredibly..."

Excited.

Thrilled.

Happy.

Yes, Todd. I know.

He steps over to another screen and keyboard. He taps on the keys, filling the truck with soft yellow light. "It's just so different now. I mean, it's a challenge, for sure. Working like this is much harder than back then. When we made you, it wasn't just me and the asshole stuck in a garbage truck. He had hundreds of scientists working for him long-distance. A separate team to manipulate the DNA, RNA, and proteins. Other experts working alongside them, engineering new genomes. And even with all that money and resources, he barely made it."

No vials clink inside me. No *confidence* evaporates from me, not that Todd really needs it. Where his task is a challenging one, the pure joy of creating, healing, and nurturing compensates for what Todd lacks in self-assurance.

He's doing this for the right reasons. His heart is in the right place.

Just like yours is now, Z.

I sit back. Close my eyes. Listen to Todd's excited blabbering.

"It's simply not enough to be an expert on synthetic organisms, cellular automata, or deep-learning systems. We need all of it. You've asked *me* to be all of it, Y. And somehow, some way, I might have done just that."

Cotton balls and satin silk. My body and brain grow warm as I watch Todd work with the hundreds of wires, tubes, and cables entering your body.

Words continue to roll off his smiling lips. He moves from the screen to you, to another screen, to the heartrate monitor, and back to you again.

When Todd's pinky finger discreetly caresses the top of your purple-red scalp, I can almost feel the touch against my own hairless skull.

At the sound of your heart beating to life, Todd's system bursts with dopamine and oxytocin. He jumps up and down. His hands cup his gasping and laughing face. His wide eyes glance at me once before he laughs even more, merging into the data on the screens.

With a smile in my eyes, I stand up from the passenger's seat by the truck's back doors. Todd's cheerful voice fills my ears. I move to the freezer. I grab a handful of electrolyte sachets and shove them into my pocket. I take a syringe from the fridge, bring it to my left arm, and insert what's inside into my system.

I glance at the operating table. Todd's folded over your body, his fingers gently separating the fine seal between your perfect, pink lips. It's a task that'll need his full attention—for at least 20.5 seconds.

With my left hand, I pull aside the clothing on my right shoulder. The knife marks and temporary stitching are evident against my blue skin. As silently as possible, I jerk the limb upward. The arm comes off clean from its ready-made seam.

I set the arm on the passenger seat.

Sidestep to Todd's computer.

Type in the letters—the first words I've ever written.

I pull on the baseball cap. Lift the metal rake jammed between the handlebars, yank it out, and slip out of the vehicle.

Todd will tell you about me. About Y, your predecessor.

Soon he'll notice I've left him. Once you're sitting upright on the operating table, your heart beating, your pink lips uttering your first, nonsensical words. And soon after, he'll notice the message on his yellow-lit computer screen:

I have gone. To feed the ants.

EPILOGUE
Z

She lifts the still-warm body above her head—and lets it plummet onto the forest floor. The torso jiggles lightly at the impact, the head landing on bare stone with a stomach-turning *crack*. Chainsaw in one hand, the blood-stained rake in the other, I wince and look away from the rainbow-colored Prototype.

Jeez, Z.

She turns to look at me, her big eyes blinking every five seconds, sharp. "Oopsie, Todd."

I force a smile. "Hey no, that's okay. Two or three hours, and the vultures will have taken care of it."

She nods. Awkwardly, she wipes her hands together. It's the first time she uses this gesture. She must have seen it on the internet, or maybe she monkeyed it from me.

Sometimes I wish you weren't so...incredibly new.

"We chop and spread, Todd."

"Yes, Z. Here." I toss the rake to her, but her body stands perfectly still as the business-end lands on her foot and the handle thwacks her on the head.

So much for the latest reflex arc update.

"Sorry, sorry, sorry!" I walk over and hand her the chainsaw. "How about you do the honors this time?"

"Honors, Todd."

"Honors means it's your turn to prepare the, uh... chow for *Canis lupus.*"

Another nod.

Her brain hasn't grasped the concept of questions yet. Just like she doesn't quite understand how brutal her handling of dead human bodies seems to another human being. Redlister or not, I have a hard time not wincing whenever we come to feed the forest animals with Z's latest red-list checkmark.

"Hey, before you begin..." I scratch the back of my neck and dodge her big, innocent eyes. Every week, I feel guilty of asking. Every week, I do it anyway. "Got any scent of her?"

Blink, five-second pause.

Blink, five-second pause.

She points her blue finger at a path leading to the cliff's edge.

"Thanks, Z. You can, uh...yeah, go ahead with the, um...meat."

I watch her grab the chainsaw and run a short

search on how to use it. A loud *rat-rat-rata-ta-ta* splits the air. Spooked birds tweet angrily, shooting from the bushes and trees to flee the monstrous sound.

The sound of the saw grinding through cartilage and bone fills my ears. Nausea growing in my stomach, I turn my back on Z and her task. Feeding the forest animals isn't something I feel strongly about. In fact, not too long ago, the only time I even thought about animals was when I taught Y their names, first in Latin, then in English. But bringing the Redlister meat here—guess it just feels like the right thing to do.

I look around the thick forest. I step onto the small path, stop. Pebbles, rock, and roots stick up from the ground. A bundle of plastic in one pocket and the syringe in the other, I head down the trail in the direction Z pointed out. One step down the path, two, three—the chainsaw's splitting sound turns into a low hum. "Todd, go."

"No, Z," I holler over my shoulder. "Not going away, just looking around. Don't worry, it's all good."

The *rat-rat-rata-ta-ta* returns. I walk down the path made of pine needles and dead leaves, scanning the young birch trees, brush, and stone boulders covered in moss. I move slowly, investigating the brush, trying to locate a swarm.

Why does it all have to look so alike...aha.

I leave the path, leaping over tall blueberries and

lush hay. At the ledge of the natural rock cliff, an enormous ant nest mounds against an oak tree.

Careful not to step on the line of ants approaching the nest—all carrying small pieces of something on their backs—I circle around the swarming mount. Finally, I locate what I was looking for.

I step closer and reach for the empty sachets of electrolytes. In a split second, three ants sink their minuscule teeth into my fingers.

Ow, you little shits...

With a quick flick of my wrist, I get rid of my assailants. I take a step back, look around for a good spot. A tree stump, covered by a thick Mapleleaf viburnum shrub. It'll do.

Viburnum acerifolium, I think and dig through my pockets. I set a bundle of electrolyte sachets and one full syringe on the stump.

I stare at the swarm of ants for a long time. How long, it's hard to say. I haven't been quite the same since she left. Sleeping, eating, especially driving—it takes the wind out of me.

I have a hard time focusing on anything but waiting to come here, hoping to see her again. The guilt and shame I feel for not bringing more syringes at one time...it grows every week. I justify withholding the syringes by telling myself how catastrophic it'd be if the birds found the syringes before her. She'd be left without. The thought that always follows next is just as bad as me skimping on the immune suppressants.

You'd be forced to come find me. Your survival instinct would bring you back home.

I shake my head, shake the thought. So far, this sort of blackmail remains beyond me. No matter how much I miss her, no matter how long I need to wait for our truck family's reunion—I won't leave her high and dry.

Won't force her hand.

I refuse to do anything other than support her way of living, no matter how mystifying her life choices are to me.

The sound of the chainsaw stops suddenly. *Three, two, one,* I count in my head until I hear Z's clear and child-like voice echoing down the path. "Invisible, Todd."

"Be right there, Z."

I give myself ten more seconds to stare at the swarming nest. Empty electrolytes closed in my fist, I shut my eyes and listen carefully. The hum of the trees is clear in my ears. The leaves rustle in the wind, the birds continue singing.

Who am I kidding? Even if you're there, watching, waiting, my mediocre human senses will never be able to locate you.

"Z's headspace bored, Todd."

A small smile twitches my lips at the sound of Z's clear voice. One last glance at this week's supply—souvenirs from her old world—and I turn around and leave. I pull a leaf from the shrubs and run my fingers on its fuzzy texture.

Viburnum acerifolium. I continue up the path and return Z's excited wave with a little laugh. *One day, when you come back. If you choose to come back. We can move on from animal names to plants.*

THE END

Shoot! The novella PROTOTYPE Y is at a close. But don't worry, you can read more fantastic fiction from Taya DeVere in the standalone novel THE ISLANDER, coming in 2025!

My dearest reader,

You are simply amazing! Thank you so much for your support and readership! I can't tell you how much you reading this book means to me. I'm humbled and honored that you've dedicated your valuable time to experience the Prototype Y universe with me. I'm still a newbie author, so if you were to leave me a review on the store you purchased this from, or Goodreads it would be a huge help! Short or long, doesn't matter. Reviews are the best way to help other readers find all of my books.

Want to stay in touch? I would love it if you'd subscribe to my newsletter:

@ www.TayaDeVere.com/HappinessProgram

You can also find me on:

Facebook.........................@TayaDeVereAuthor

Instagram.........................@TayaDeVere_Author

Goodreads.........................@TayaDeVere

Bookbub.........................@Taya-DeVere

Gratefully yours,
Taya

About the Author

Taya DeVere is a Finnish science fiction writer who loves telling stories about perfectly imperfect people in dystopian and postapocalyptic settings. Her characters are outsiders and rebels who stand up against injustice and form unlikely friendships with other rebels along the way. She is the writer of more than 21 books, and is always developing new stories to delight her readers. Taya's restless feet have taken her all over Finland, the United Kingdom, Spain, and North America. She lived in the United States for seven years but is currently based in Turku, Finland with her partner, Chris.

Best things in life: friends & family, memories made, and mistakes to learn from. Taya also loves licorice ice cream, secondhand clothes and things, bunny sneezes, salmiakki, and sauna.

Dislikes: clowns, the Muppets, Moomin trolls, dolls (especially porcelain dolls), human size mascots, and celery.

Taya's writing is inspired by the works of authors like Margaret Atwood, Octavia E. Butler, Hugh Howey, and Blake Crouch.

Final Thanks

What. A. Ride. When I first outlined the Unchipped story and realized I was looking at a twenty-book series, I didn't know what I was getting myself into. But surely enough, after the first draft of the first book, the Unchipped story grew legs, and the characters snatched the reins from me. I can't tell you how many notes I took in the middle of the night, as I once again woke up to an idea for a scene or a snippet of dialogue.

Final Thanks

[illegible]

www.ingramcontent.com/pod-product-compliance
Ingram Content Group UK Ltd.
Pitfield, Milton Keynes, MK11 3LW, UK
UKHW040625030625
6203UKWH00023B/382
9 789527 601068